THE BODY AT BALA LAKE

A NESTA GRIFFITHS MYSTERY

P. L. HANDLEY

CHAPTER 1

Hari whimpered with his nose pressed up against the kitchen floor. He tilted back his head to find a figure towering above him and stared at it with pleading eyes.

"Alright, fine. You win."

Nesta Griffiths grabbed the lead from her kitchen table and sent the eager Jack Russell Terrier spinning into an excited frenzy. She shook her head, as her dog began jumping up and down like a hairy bouncy ball.

"Calm down," she said. "Or you'll hurt yourself."

The ageing canine paid little attention to his owner's advice and continued bouncing off the walls until they had escaped through the front door.

It was a sunny May bank holiday weekend in the little town of Bala and most of its residents were still tucked up in bed at such an early hour. An exception to these people was Nesta Griffiths, who had been forced out of the house by a very impatient and rather tenacious Jack Russell.

Bala was situated beside the largest natural lake in Wales, and the retired teacher had lived in the area all of her life. Still, this familiarity had not prevented her from appreciating the timeless beauty of her rural surroundings, and, having lost her husband only three years ago, these walks with Hari had been an important part of her daily routine. Maintaining a sense of structure had played a vital part in securing *some* sense of normality in her life. In fact, had it not been for her loyal, furry friend, she probably would have stayed indoors for days on end.

"Keep busy," had been her late husband's motto, which was rather ironic for a local police officer in the heart of Snowdonia. Sergeant Morgan Griffiths had been stationed in Bala for his entire career and had been well-respected within his local community. It wasn't easy keeping the peace in a town where everyone knew each other. In a population that spread itself out across miles of elevated land, everyone knew everyone. Morgan had very rarely discussed his work at home, but Nesta was certain that her husband had at least experienced *some* action during his time on the force (like the time a farmer named Dilwyn had accidentally shot off his own toe).

If she had been completely honest, Nesta had always been a little jealous of her husband's profession. It wasn't that she hadn't enjoyed her career teaching secondary school English (although, if she had been forced to discuss the themes *Of Mice and Men* one more time, she would have torn the book up and tossed it into the lake), but she had also harboured her own desires of solving crimes. Perhaps it was her love for Agatha Christie, or her fascination with true crime stories, or, most likely, it was probably her secret desire to try on a stab vest and carry around a truncheon — but the less said about that, the better. Either way, she had always regretted not sending off the application form.

There was a great sense of calm and tranquillity that morning on Nesta's stroll along the narrow shoreline. The lake known as Llyn Tegid was like a pane of reflective glass facing up towards a clear, blue sky. All was still, and the only sound was the crunching of gravel beneath her feet.

Nesta looked out across the water towards the Aran Fawddwy mountain that loomed across the tiny village of Llanuwchllyn on the other side of the lake. It was a view that she had never grown tired of, and everything in her peripheral vision was exactly as it had appeared every morning — all except one small difference.

As she moved closer in the direction of a stone jetty, the bright purple object became more and more visible with every step. Hari let out a series of loud barks, and Nesta cupped her mouth. The retired teacher realised very quickly that she was in fact looking at the body of a male adult.

The lifeless figure stared back at her with a pair of vacant eyes. She gasped for a second time and saw that the face was one she recognised; it was a person that she had known since her years of teaching at Bala Secondary School. As someone who had been so full of life during his youth, the man was now, quite literally, a shell of his former self.

"Dafydd Thomas," Nesta muttered under her breath. She had not uttered *that* name in quite some time.

The retired teacher stood there, staring at her former pupil for what had felt like an eternity. By the time she had made the short walk over to the police station, Nesta had begun to wonder whether she had imagined the entire thing.

Constable Aled Parry had only just started his shift when she arrived at the front counter, and he had presumed that the wife of his former sergeant was there for another one of her little social visits. It was then that she broke the news.

"You should have called me straight away," he said, scrambling for his coat.

"This *is* me calling you straight away," said Nesta.

"I mean, on your mobile phone."

"I don't have a mobile phone."

The young police officer stared at her as though she was dressed in prehistoric furs and carrying a wooden club. "How can you not have a —" He didn't bother finishing his question and hurried her into his police car.

"It's only a ten-minute walk," Nesta said, as her driver fired up the engine.

"There's no time to lose," said Aled.

Nesta wanted to point out that, had she not have stumbled upon the body in the first place, Dafydd Thomas would still be lying there for at least another hour or so. After all, it wasn't like he was going anywhere. But she didn't think her words would make the highly-stressed man feel any better at this point, and they sat in silence for the entire minute it had taken to drive back to the lake.

Constable Parry had barely completed his second year in the job and was finding his new life as a fully-fledged man-of-the-law a lot more stressful than he had first expected. Had he known how much administration and paperwork was involved, he might have gone with his second option of becoming a qualified carpenter.

"Over there," said Nesta, as they pulled up into the lakeview car park.

Aled followed her pointed finger towards the figure lying in the gravel. His entire body went numb, and his hands began to tremble. "Right," he said. "You stay in the car, Mrs Griffiths."

"But —"

"I need to secure the area — wait — no! I should check if he's actually dead."

"Oh, he's definitely dead," said Nesta with a sigh.

"Yes, but I need to see it for myself." Aled opened his door and hesitated. He was getting more pale with every passing second.

"Are you sure you don't want us to come with you?"

The police officer looked over at Nesta and the curious Jack Russell sitting in the footwell.

"Actually," he said. "Yes, I think you better had. Just to confirm the identity."

Nesta rolled her eyes and followed the young man down to the narrow shore. They both stood over the body with the same disturbed expression.

Aled knelt down and placed his finger near Dafydd's neck.

"You won't find his pulse there," said Nesta.

"I know where his pulse is!" Aled snapped. He saw the woman's surprised face and took a deep breath to calm himself down. "I'm sorry, Mrs Griffiths. I didn't mean to —"

Before he could finish his sentence, the constable cupped his mouth and turned around. The heaving sound made Nesta cringe. "It's alright, Aled," she said.

Aled stood up again and dried his mouth. "Well, I think he's definitely dead."

The woman beside him nodded. "I think you'd better call this one in, Aled."

The police officer began searching for his police radio as though he had lost his house keys. "Yes, I think that's probably a good idea."

Whilst Aled began making the first step of turning this peaceful location into a busy crime scene, Nesta looked over at the Maserati sports car parked nearby. Apart from the police car, it was the only other vehicle in sight, and she presumed it belonged to the deceased. She took one last look at Dafydd Thomas' hollow expression and shuddered. It was a sight that would be haunting her dreams for quite some time.

CHAPTER 2

"Dafydd Thomas?!"

"Keep your voice down," said Nesta with a *hush*. She looked around at the busy chip shop. *The Badell Aur* on Bala High Street was a regular meeting point for her little catch-ups with Catrin Jones. The woman in her mid-thirties was now the local secondary school's deputy headteacher, and, despite the age difference, she had formed an unlikely friendship with her former mentor.

Nesta had retired only a few years after Catrin had started her first job, yet the more experienced teacher had made quite an impression before she left. Teaching a class full of secondary school pupils had been a daunting task for someone who was practically an adolescent herself, and she had never forgotten Nesta's support during those difficult times.

In many ways, Nesta Griffiths had become somewhat of a role model and someone she continued to channel in the later stage of her career.

Nesta had enjoyed watching her unofficial protégé grow and mature over the years. Catrin had always been far stronger than *she* had been during her early twenties (not that she would ever admit it to her), and she had seen her potential from the very first day.

"Everyone probably already knows by now," said Catrin, who appeared to be still taking in the news. "Dafydd Thomas... I still can't believe it." She shook her head before being struck by another thought. "Oh, you know what I'm thinking next —"

"You need a new sports teacher?" asked Nesta.

"Nesta!" Catrin cried. "That's not funny."

Nesta shrugged and stirred her tea. "You will, though."

"Yes, but I'm not *that* cold-hearted."

"You were back when I was teaching." The older woman gave her friend a playful smirk.

Catrin merely shook her head again in disapproval. "I was thinking about his poor fiancée. She'll be devastated."

"He was getting married?" asked Nesta, raising an eyebrow. If there was one place the police looked first in a murder investigation, she thought, it was the partner. Unlike her treasured murder mystery books, real-life murders were a lot more straightforward. Most people, provided they were of sound mind, did not tend to plan out their other half's demise, and were far more likely to strike their partner down in the heat of a volatile argument. Thoughts like this were often circling around Nesta's mind, and she often wondered whether she needed to read a little less crime fiction.

"Dafydd was supposed to be getting married to Donna Lloyd at the end of the summer," Catrin continued. "He's been talking about it for months."

"Donna Lloyd," said Nesta with a nod. She remembered that pupil well. Donna had possessed a sharp mind and, at times, an even sharper tongue. Her former student was, Nesta had decided, far too clever for her own good sometimes. She was a grade-A student, but all whilst barely having to put in the effort. Had she put as much effort into her studying as she did her social life, the young woman would have had a bright future ahead of her.

"Childhood sweethearts," said Catrin with a sad smile. "We were all so pleased for them."

"Yes," Nesta said. "Now that you mention it, I *do* remember those two together. They couldn't keep their hands off each other."

Catrin listened to the older woman, as she tutted away. "You never did strike me as the hopeless romantic."

Nesta let out a grunt. "When you've studied Shakespeare as much as I have, you get very tired of that word."

"Romance?" Catrin leant forward with a mischievous face. "You're telling me Morgan never swooped you off your feet? That he never grabbed you in a moment of uncontrollable passion?" She couldn't help but giggle.

Nesta rolled her eyes. "I was lucky if he left me the last chocolate *Hobnob* biscuit."

The younger woman sprayed out some of her tea in a burst of laughter and had to dry her friend's forehead with a napkin. "Sorry," she said. "I couldn't help it."

"Give me a good crime novel over a romance book anyday," said Nesta with a sigh.

"Sounds like we've got a real murder mystery on our hands now," said Catrin. She sipped on the rest of her tea and shuddered. "Oh, God, what am I going to tell the pupils?"

"That's not really your job." Nesta cringed at the thought of who was now in charge of her old school. "It should be announced by the headteacher."

Catrin cringed herself. "Well, yes, but you know what *he's* like. Either way, it'll end up falling on me."

Nesta had been in complete shock when she first discovered the identity of *Bala Secondary School*'s new headteacher. John Glyn was the youngest headmaster in the school's history and seemed to be more interested in being popular than he was about the welfare of his staff and pupils. At least, this was Nesta's opinion. Like most of the people in Bala under the age of forty, she had taught this young man for many years. He had been a keen footballer, and, had he been offered a contract at *Liverpool Football Club* over teaching the youth of his hometown, he would have taken the first option in an instant.

"How he got that job I'll never know," Nesta muttered.

"I think we both know why," said Catrin.

"Because he's a man?"

The deputy headteacher laughed, only this time her mouth was empty. "Because he was the only one who wanted it," she said. "Nobody else in that staff room wanted to take on that job. It's easier being the prime minister."

"You mean, nobody else is *stupid* enough to take that job?"

"Well, yes, perhaps. I think Johnny was just looking for extra money. He's still paying off that sports car he can't afford."

"Johnny?" Nesta asked.

Catrin smirked. "That's what he calls himself now."

The retired teacher rolled her eyes. "Of course he does."

"The man just doesn't seem to understand what the role entails," said Catrin, stirring her tea with a hopeless gaze. "I'm sure he will in time."

Nesta scoffed. "You're a lot more optimistic than me. He's very lucky to have a person like you as his deputy. I'm just glad I left before that numpty took over the throne."

Catrin paused and began awkwardly fidgeting with her napkin. "Actually, that reminds me. There's something I wanted to ask you." The other woman looked up with a feeling of dread, as though, by an act of telepathy, she knew what the question was going to be. "How do you feel about coming back?" The retired teacher did not reply and merely stared at her. "I don't mean full time or anything. Just a few days here and there."

Nesta remained cynical and pushed her half-eaten plate of food away. "You're asking me to be a supply teacher?"

"It's very flexible," Catrin added quickly. "Teachers do it all the time after they retire. Annie Proctor still comes back."

The older woman continued to stare, until she let out a deep sigh. "Are you asking? Or begging?"

Catrin unleashed a sigh of her own and held her head in shame. "Alright, I'm begging. It would really help us out. We already have one teacher on maternity leave, and we're down a physics teacher."

"And a sports teacher," said Nesta, who couldn't help but look smug.

"Oh, yeah. I forgot about that."

Nesta sat back in her chair and gave the proposition some thought. She had enjoyed her retirement at first, but it wasn't long before she started craving a new challenge. "Don't think you'll be finding me running around that playing field in a tracksuit and blowing a whistle."

Catrin smiled. "Don't worry, I wouldn't do that to you. You wouldn't be covering physical education. Although... I *can* imagine you with a whistle."

Nesta grinned. "I *would* quite enjoy a whistle." She pictured herself barking at the pupils like a sergeant major.

"So what do you say?" asked Catrin, before a painful silence caused her to be even more nervous.

"I'll think about it."

The deputy headteacher groaned. "It's not like you've got anything else to do."

Nesta was almost offended. "I'll have you know that I've got a reading list that's the length of that lake out there. And a dog to walk. Plus, I've started pilates now." She paused to think about it. "Or is it yoga?" In the end, she shook her head. "Well, I've filled out the joining form, anyway."

Catrin folded up her arms in a sulk. "Well, I'd better not keep you any longer, then. You'll miss *Loose Women* soon."

"Don't talk daft," the retired woman snapped. "*Loose Women* is only on during the week."

They both smiled at each other and reached for their coats. As Catrin stood up, she noticed something going on through the large window behind her friend.

"Hello," she said. "*Someone*'s in trouble."

Nesta turned around to see a police car parked outside *The Plas Coch Hotel* pub. Two officers were making their way inside through the main doors. "Do you think it's regarding Dafydd Thomas?" she asked.

Catrin turned to her friend in surprise. "What makes you think that?"

Nesta shrugged. "The police will be busy making their usual enquiries. Seems like there's a link to the pub."

"You really think so?" asked Catrin.

"A good detective will always start with the most obvious connections," said Nesta. "Maybe the man had his drink poisoned. Or worse yet, perhaps he was drugged and killed later on."

The deputy head shuddered at the mere thought of it. "You have a warped mind, Nesta Griffiths."

The retired teacher looked back at the pub with its red-painted exterior and Welsh flag drooping down above the door. "Either that," she said, "or the police are now drinking on the job."

Without saying another word, they both headed towards the door. Before leaving her favourite chip shop, Nesta turned around to see the various heads of feasting locals. She recognised almost everyone but was now seeing them in a completely new light. Suddenly, every resident in her hometown was now a potential murder suspect. There was no proof that Dafydd

Thomas really *had* been murdered, of course, but there was still a possibility. The prospect of there being a killer on the loose gave Nesta a slight chill down the back of her neck, but, if she was *really* being honest, it also filled her with an unexpected rush of excitement.

CHAPTER 3

Nestled in the middle of the A494, the town of Bala was a place that many travellers would deem the perfect stopping-off point on a scenic drive through the heart of North Wales. The local residents of this community would not dispute this idea, but they also knew that their historic town was far more than just an idyllic spot for some ice cream and chips.

Bala was the central hub of an area that stretched out across multiple surrounding villages, a place where people could be reacquainted with old friends whilst topping up on a few essential grocery items.

For Nesta Griffiths, walking down the town's bustling high street was about as difficult as finding an empty parking space, and she could barely make a few footsteps without bumping into at least one familiar face. In a town where everyone knew your name, it wasn't easy getting a weekly shopping list ticked off in a timely manner, and that day, having decided to brave the rush of her local butcher shop, was no different. After two conversations about the lack of sunshine and two more about the infuriating decision-making of the local council, she had finally made it as far as the town's famous monument.

The statue of Thomas Edward Ellis, a notable Welsh politician, stood tall outside the *Awen Meirion* book shop. This bronze figure raised his hand up into the sky with the same hollow expression as the teenager sitting against its chamfered base. Darren Price looked up from his mobile phone and caught the steely gaze of the woman approaching him, before he returned to the comfort of his screen.

"Is that yours?"

Darren looked up again to find Nesta pointing down towards an empty *Coke* can near his feet. The teenager ignored her question with a snort.

"Is that yours?" Nesta asked again with a raised voice. It was a tone she had long perfected over her teaching career and was a sure-fire way to get any person's attention.

The fifteen-year-old sighed and adjusted the hood over his long, dark hair. "So what if it is?"

The former teacher felt her body temperature rise. Her words had failed to instil their usual effect, and the respect she had been used to commanding within the hallways of *Bala Secondary School* was nowhere to be seen on the high street.

"Would it kill you to walk a couple of feet?" She pointed towards the nearby rubbish bin.

"It's not even mine," said Darren, failing to take his attention off the phone.

Nesta let out a sigh of her own and marched over to pick up the empty can.

Darren heard the item *clank* into the bottom of the rubbish bin and couldn't help but smile.

"Don't you have anything better to do than loiter around here all day?" Nesta asked.

"I'm quite busy, actually." The teenager pointed at his device and continued to pound away at it with his fingertips.

The retired teacher let out a long groan. "Thank goodness they didn't have those wretched things in my day. Or there would have been a pile of them outside my classroom window."

Darren took a quick glance at her and smirked. "When was that? Victorian times?"

Just as Nesta let out a furious shudder, she caught a glimpse at the face underneath the black hoodie. "Wait," she said. "You're Gwyn Price's boy!"

The teenager's smug expression had morphed into one of sudden discomfort. He much preferred to go about his business with as little human interaction as possible — let alone have someone recognise him.

"Nah," said Darren. "Sorry, you got the wrong guy."

Nesta shook her head and bent her knees to get a better look underneath his hood. "I'd recognise that chin anywhere. You're the spitting image." She watched the teenager cringe. "Yes, I remember your father well. He was ever so well behaved — bright too! I hear he's got his very own solicitors office in Chester."

Darren slumped down until he resembled a gargoyle on the side of the monument. "You must be very proud," he muttered. "What a legend."

The retired teacher noticed the resentment in his face and studied him like a sheet of paper with tiny text. "What would your father make of you being out here on the streets?"

"The streets?" Darren asked with a snigger. "Take a look around — this is hardly downtown Detroit." His amused expression turned sour again. "Besides, it's not like my old man would ever notice. He's forty miles away in a different country."

"It's only Chester," said Nesta. "And surely he's not working on a Saturday?"

"He works everyday." The teenager folded up his arms. "Which is fine by me. I'm used to taking care of myself."

Despite the young man's obnoxious tone, Nesta couldn't help but feel a slight tinge of sympathy. She had heard about his parents' separation and had experienced a similar pain herself after the loss of her father at the age of twelve. His terminal illness had rocked the entire family and had left her mother to raise three children single-handedly.

"I'm sorry about what happened with your parents," she said, eventually. "How's your mother?"

The teenager looked up, surprised for a moment, until he remembered where he lived. Everybody knew everything in this town.

"Living the dream," Darren muttered.

"How do you mean?"

Darren pointed towards the high street. "She escaped this place, didn't she?"

"I heard she moved to Warrington."

"Runcorn."

Nesta sighed and nodded. "And what do you intend to do with your life?"

The teenager shook his head. He could tell that she used to be a teacher. It was easy to spot one a mile off, he thought. They never seemed to switch off — not even when they were retired. "I'm getting as far away from here as I can," he said. "There's no way I'm staying in this town."

"What's so bad about Bala?" Nesta asked. She was genuinely curious. Having lived in the town all of her life, the born-and-bred local could not have imagined living anywhere else.

Darren gave her a cynical stare. "Come on. Surely, I don't need to explain that."

"Try me."

The teenager sat up and lowered his hood to reveal a head

full of long, jet-black hair. His complexion was pale, like someone who rarely ventured outdoors unless he had to. "I want to live in a place where people mind their own flaming business." He waited for her to take the hint, but his comment didn't seem blunt enough.

"We've got a post office," said Nesta. "And a *Co-op*. What more do you need?"

Darren scoffed and returned to his mobile phone.

"You won't be going anywhere if you keep melting your brain with that thing," she added.

The young man lifted up his electronic device and smirked. "This is my ticket out of here." Nesta waited for him to elaborate. She couldn't wait to hear him explain *this* one. "I'm going to be a professional influencer."

The retired teacher went blank. "A *what*?"

Darren sighed. "An influencer! A social media star."

The woman standing opposite him was none the wiser. "Social — what?"

"A *YouTube* star." He lifted up his phone. "I've started my own channel."

Nesta peered down at the screen and slipped on her glasses. She could see a video of Darren staring into the lens from the comfort of his own bed. Why anyone would ever want to watch such a thing, she would never know.

"Is that you?" she asked.

"No," said Darren. "It's Justin Bieber."

"It's who?"

"Yes, it's me!"

Nesta continued to stare at the screen as though she were trying to read a slate of ancient calligraphy. "What does that number mean?"

"It's how many views I've had," Darren replied with a proud grin.

"Twenty-six?" Nesta asked. She waited for the nod and patted the young man on the back. "Well, good luck with that. I'm sure you'll be rich and famous in no time. Maybe, in the meantime, you should try reading something."

The former teacher shook her head and continued her walk down the high street.

"Maybe you should try minding your own business," Darren muttered, but only when she was safely out of earshot.

The butcher shop at the end of the high street was as busy as Nesta had expected. Her only hope was that she hadn't missed out on the establishment's famous sausage rolls, which she always enjoyed eating on her way home.

"Don't you burn my tongue again," she said, giving the adolescent shop assistant a threatening glare from the other side of the counter.

The young butcher rolled his eyes, as he grabbed the penultimate sausage roll and went to heat it up in the back room.

Nesta waited amongst the crowd of customers with her weekly meat shop now safely wrapped up in her large bag. As she stared down at the selection of pork chops lining the glass counter, a pair of voices chatted away behind her.

"It's mental, isn't it?"

"Surely, it wasn't *murder*."

"Look, it says it right here on the *Daily Post* website — the police are treating the death as highly suspicious. The article only went up online half an hour ago."

Nesta turned around to see two women gathered around a mobile phone. She recognised them both and, not surprisingly, had taught both of their parents.

"It's there in black and white," said Delyth, a local midwife with fiery red hair.

"God, you're right." Iola, a woman who worked over at the

bank, peered into the faint light coming from her friend's phone. "He must have been killed."

The retired teacher in front of them did her best to get a better look at the phone and tilted her head from side to side like a curious ostrich. Unfortunately, and especially with *her* eyesight, there was no chance that she was going to get a proper look, and Nesta continued to bob and weave until a piping-hot sausage roll hovered into her periphery.

"Oh," she said, slightly embarrassed, as the young shop assistant handed her the pastry.

Moments later, and Nesta was marching back down the high street at a frantic pace. The teenager still perched against the old monument didn't even get a chance to see her coming, before she grabbed hold of his phone.

"Hey!" he cried out in protest.

The woman began fondling the device as if it had dropped out of a passing spaceship and eventually gave up. "How do you check the news on this thing?" she asked, handing it back to its disgruntled owner.

"What would you want to check the news for?" asked Darren, rubbing his phone to check for scratch marks.

"To nourish your brain," Nesta snapped (not that she really considered the news to be a decent source of education anyway, but it was more than what the teenager was surely getting on "You-Hoo-Tube").

"Get your own phone," Darren snapped back.

"I don't need another phone," said Nesta. "I've already got a cordless landline in my kitchen. What I need right now is to check the *Daily Post*'s latest article."

"What for?"

The woman sighed. "To read about the murder."

Unintentionally, and in a single sentence, she had piqued the teenager's interest. "*Murder*? What murder?"

Nesta gave him a frustrated frown. "Maybe, if you bring up the article on your little *Gameboy* machine, you'll find out."

Darren rolled his eyes and let curiosity get the better of him. In a matter of seconds, the newspaper article was up on his small screen, and both of them were gathered around it like campers in front of a tiny fire.

"Mr Thomas?" Darren eventually asked. "He's *dead*?"

Nesta turned her gaze away from the screen and stared at him. "Have you been living under a rock? The whole town's been talking about it all morning."

The teenager cringed. "The whole town needs to get a life."

After finishing the last paragraph, Nesta moved away from the device and prayed that she didn't end up catching some horrible virus from its electronic rays. "So, it's official — Dafydd Thomas has been murdered."

Darren seemed surprisingly pleased. "Great. That hopefully means no more sports lessons."

The retired teacher shook her head in disapproval at his heartless comment. "A man has just been killed, and all you're worried about is avoiding a little physical activity."

"I never liked the guy anyway," Darren muttered. "He wouldn't even let me wear jeans."

"You wear jeans to do sports in?" Nesta asked in shock.

"I cut them down into shorts," the teenager replied, raising his arms in the air as though it was perfectly normal. "I hate football. Can't stand rugby. And I don't like running."

"Are there any sports you *do* like?"

Darren gave her question some thought. "Skateboarding." He could feel the woman's judgement without even looking at her. "Why are you so interested in this story, anyway? People die all the time. I thought you'd be used to it."

Nesta snapped her head around to glare at him. "What do you mean by that?"

The teenager shrugged. "You get older, people die more."

The woman beside him let out a grunt. The only thing worse than his rude comment was the fact that he was also right. She had lost a few people in her life over the last few years, but she didn't need some obnoxious teenager to remind her of that.

"Where are you going?" Darren asked, as she began walking away from him.

"Where do you think I'm going?" she called out. "To get my ham in the fridge."

CHAPTER 4

If the butcher shop at the top end of Bala high street had been like *Selfridges* during a Boxing Day sale, then the inside of *The Plas Coch Hotel* was as quiet as a carvery buffet during the pandemic. It was, after all, still early doors, and in a few hours, the pub would be packed full of punters from all over the surrounding area. Until then, however, the only presence at this hour was a lonely figure who sat at the bar, gazing at the unfamiliar drink bottles.

Nesta had never been much of a drinker and couldn't remember the last time she had stepped inside *The Plas Coch*. The pubs in her hometown had a certain reputation for being quite rowdy on a Friday and Saturday night, with the youth of the nearby villages and farms having chosen these watering holes as the perfect places to let their hair down. It was hardly the Vegas Strip, but there were at least a handful of pubs for them to rotate around until the sound of the last orders bell.

The retired teacher much preferred to enjoy her occasional glass of wine in the comfort of her own living room, preferably with a dose of *Strictly Come Dancing* (not that she would tell anyone). On this Saturday lunchtime, she had made a rare exception, and nobody was more surprised than barmaid Sioned Tudor.

"Mrs Griffiths?" Sioned asked, as she came walking into the bar area with a fresh pack of tonic waters. The sight of her former teacher sitting at the bar had almost been enough for her to drop the entire pack. "What are you doing here?"

Nesta looked around the pub with an innocent face. "I'm doing what any normal person would do in a place like this. Buying a drink. Is that a crime?"

The barmaid placed the container down and moved suspiciously towards the till. "As long as you're not here to teach me Shakespeare," she said.

The older woman rolled her eyes. "I didn't have much luck with that in a dedicated classroom. What makes you think I'd have a better chance in here?"

"Get a few gin and tonics inside of you and maybe you might find out," said Sioned with a playful grin.

Nesta sighed. "Charming as ever."

Sioned lifted up a bottle of cognac from the shelf behind her and lifted it up as though it were a human skull. "To be drunk, or not to be drunk: that is the question."

Her audience of one witnessed her impromptu performance with a cynical frown. "Hamlet. Very nice."

"That was Hamlet?" Sioned asked. "I can't wait to tell the other half that I just quoted *Hamlet*. He'll be well impressed."

"I can only imagine."

The barmaid leant against one of the beer pumps. "So what can I get you, Mrs Griffiths?"

"You know that you can call me Nesta?"

Sioned shook her head. "Nah. Doesn't feel right. Just too weird."

"I'll have a Bloody Mary," Nesta muttered.

Her server jumped into action, and, very shortly, there was a full glass of pink-red liquid in her hand.

"So what *really* brings you in here?" Sioned asked, wiping the bar down with her cloth. "Are you waiting for a hot date?"

"I wish," said Nesta with a smile. She could already feel the vodka working its magic.

The barmaid giggled. "Give it a couple of hours. If you like a farmer in a rugby shirt, this place will be full of them. Although I can't promise you any lookers. And they can get a bit wild after a few beers."

"That's why I married a policeman," said the older woman. "I much prefer the sensible type."

Sioned lit up with excitement. "Man in uniform, eh?" She tapped a finger against her own nose. "I know where you're coming from. I married a fireman."

Nesta nodded. She could certainly approve of a fireman. "Talking of people in uniform," she said, looking around to make sure they were still alone. "I noticed you had a pair of police officers in here earlier."

The barmaid groaned. "So *that's* why you came in here! Just couldn't resist another man of the law, Mrs Griffiths?"

"Something like that," said Nesta. Her plan of steering the conversation in a certain direction was working perfectly, and she had done it quicker than expected. "So what did they come in here for?"

Sioned was suddenly a little suspicious. "What makes you so interested?"

The retired teacher slurped her drink with an innocent twinkle in her eyes. "Oh, you know. Just curious. I married a police officer, remember? I miss hearing all the gossip."

"Well," said Sioned, who had secretly been dying to share her little encounter with the police. She had never been able to keep a secret. "They were asking about an altercation that happened here yesterday afternoon."

"Go on," said Nesta, twirling her finger around the rim of her glass.

"There was a fight that broke out between two men. One of them got a right slap in the face, and by slap, I mean *proper* mouthful of knuckles, like." Sioned began mimicking the blow with her own hand. "I had to get right in there and break it all up." She let out an excited grin. "It was brilliant!"

"Who were the two men involved?" asked Nesta.

"One of them was Geraint Owen — the one who landed the punch."

The older woman nodded. She knew Geraint Owen's entire family tree. The Owens had been farming the land around Fedw Glas Farm for generations. These days, it was Geraint who resided in the hundred-acre property with his young family and in a holding that could be found only a mile outside of Bala. If Nesta remembered rightly, Geraint's father, Hedd, was also known to be partial to the occasional pub brawl.

"And the other?" she asked.

"Dafydd Thomas."

The name gave Nesta a similar tingle in her throat as the tomato-based drink she was consuming. "Interesting," she said. "Any idea what the fight was about?"

Sioned scoffed. "The usual, I imagine. Probably the same reason any fight breaks out around here: testosterone, jealousy, too much alcohol, arm wrestles..."

"*Arm wrestle?*"

The barmaid shrugged. "Some of the punters like to arm wrestle come ten o'clock. It's usually if they haven't pulled and need to express themselves. A real fight tends to follow no matter what the outcome. Go figure."

Some things never change, Nesta thought. "Did you see Geraint and Dafydd talking to each other beforehand?"

Sioned shook her head. "Didn't have time. It was only me and Carys on that shift. I was fuming. It was supposed to be my night off until Eryl called and asked me to do a favour. Forgot to mention that it would be just the two of us, though, didn't he? He didn't even bother to come in himself. Selfish git."

Nesta pretended to listen, but she was secretly deep in thought. "What time was the fight?" she asked.

"It was only about five," said Sioned.

"On a Friday?" asked Nesta. "That's early to be very drunk."

"Not for some." Sioned greeted a new punter with a forced smile. "Alright, Twm? Pint of the usual? I'll bring it over."

The old man with an enormous beard nodded and took his regular spot in the corner of the room.

Sioned began pouring a fresh pint of lager whilst lowering her voice to speak with Nesta. "People like Twm come in as soon as we open. They drink all day. Sometimes I wonder if he ever eats. There's a few in here like him. They keep me company on the weekdays."

Nesta glanced at the old man with his newspaper. In some ways, she could imagine how such a habit could form. At her age, passing the time wasn't easy when you lived alone and no longer had to work. Fortunately for her, it was *Yorkshire Tea* that had been *her* drink of choice to guzzle away from morning until night, and her liver probably thanked her for it.

"But Dafydd Thomas was a teacher," she said, staring into the foam on Twm's beer. "He must have come here straight from school to be drunk by five."

"You heard what happened to him, right?" Sioned glared at her, as she strolled off to deliver the pint of beer. On her return journey back to the bar, her mischievous smile had not altered.

Nesta nodded.

"Couldn't believe it when I found out," Sioned continued, leaning down against the bar and gazing towards an empty table over by the window. "I mean, the guy was right there less than twenty-four hours ago. I saw him with my very own eyes, living and breathing. It's crazy."

"Was he alone?" asked Nesta.

Sioned nodded. "He was really knocking them back, too. Must have had a hard day at school. Don't blame him, actually. I hated school. Couldn't imagine being there as an adult." She turned to the woman on the other side of the bar and remembered who she was talking to. "Sorry, no offence."

"None taken." Nesta clutched her empty glass and tried to resist the urge for another drink. "What about Geraint? Was he alone?"

"Geraint was out with some friends," said Sioned. "They all play for the local rugby team."

"Weren't Dafydd and Geraint friends? I seem to remember them being as thick as thieves at school."

Sioned gave it some thought and nodded. "Yeah, that's true, actually. I'd forgotten about that. They were all in the same circle. Dafydd left Bala when he went off to university, though, and didn't come back here until recently."

"I suppose absence didn't make the heart grow fonder in this case," said Nesta.

"Nah," said Sioned. "Those two were like strangers yesterday. But there was a lot of tension there, too."

"In what way?"

"I don't know. Dafydd seemed to be acting like a bit of a snob. Even with me. You wouldn't know that we used to sit next to each other in geography. I suppose the p-word comes to mind."

Nesta appreciated her careful use of language. She had received the image quite clearly. "That probably didn't do him any favours with Geraint and company. Who made the first move?"

"Hard to say," said Sioned. "Although, I saw Dafydd give Geraint a shove, so I guess he had the punch coming." She looked down at Nesta's empty glass. "Can I get you another?"

The retired woman shook her head and began trying to figure out the most elegant way to leap off her uncomfortable stool. It turned out that there wasn't one, and she bid the barmaid a farewell.

When Nesta re-emerged through *The Plas Coch Hotel* doors, she was relieved to discover that it was still daylight and gazed over towards the statue on the other side of the road. The space where Darren Price had been leaning against was now empty, and, in some ways, she was relieved about that, too.

"Good lad," she muttered to herself.

CHAPTER 5

The pupils of Year Seven sat behind their desks, staring at the substitute teacher standing there before them. Not a single one of them recognised this school veteran, and most of them already missed their usual music teacher, who was probably half this woman's age.

Nesta continued her long speech about the wonders of seventeenth-century Baroque music and couldn't help but notice the audience of blank faces.

"I'm sorry," she said. "Is this too basic for you? You'll have to forgive my level of detail on this subject. My knowledge of music only stretches so far, but today it will have to do."

A pupil called Elgan raised his hand.

"Yes," said Nesta.

"Mr Harris normally lets us mess about with them lot," said Elgan, pointing towards the assortment of musical instruments in the corner of the room.

The substitute teacher cleared her throat. "He lets you play instruments? Surely there must be some theory involved. There's only so much you can learn with the practical side."

A student called Casey raised up another hand. "He says

music is about expression, Miss. Mr Harris used to say Led Zeppelin never spent all their time studying sheet music. Whoever they are."

The teacher tried to hide her horror. She was already getting a very clear picture of this Mr Harris, and he was beginning to sound more like a failed musician than a professional educator. "I'm sure Bach and Puccini would highly disagree with that statement." She saw the teenager's confused expression and sighed. "Please tell me that you've heard of Puccini?" The silence said it all. "Very well," she eventually said. "Why don't you all demonstrate what you would *normally* be doing in this class. Enlighten me. I'm dying to get an insight into Mr Harris' unique teaching methods."

Five minutes later, and the entire class was spread out across the room, each with their chosen instrument. To the teacher's dismay, it had turned out that the vast majority of the instruments were of the percussion variety, and her sensitive eardrums were soon struck by a wall of uncontrollable noise.

The pupils continued to bash away at their glockenspiels and cowbells, as a dozen recorders squeaked away to accompany them. Nesta had the urge to cover up her ears and was beginning to highly question the decision to return to teaching. At least her former syllabus of Shakespeare and Dickens didn't give her a migraine, she thought.

Once the torture of her first lesson back at *Bala Secondary School* was over, she spent a portion of her lunch break wandering the empty halls on a trip down memory lane. Not much had changed since she had left, at least, not in terms of the architecture. With every pupil now safely herded outside, she was free to explore the building in peace.

The lines of classroom doors all brought back flashes of nostalgia, mainly for the teachers who once occupied them. Many of these former comrades had now retired and left, and their ghosts lived on in Nesta's head. She would never forget old grumpy Robin Mellon, who spent the majority of his spare time locked away in his car, listening to the cricket at any given opportunity — or the socially-awkward Helen Bailey, who used to keep an endless supply of chocolate Minstrels in her desk drawer to graze on when nobody was watching.

As she approached the end of her private tour, Nesta reached a large window overlooking the school playing fields. Pupils were dotted across the grass in their groups of social circles, whilst others kicked around a football.

Over in the distance, a lonely figure was sitting by himself against an enormous oak tree. A pair of headphones covered his ears, and his wild, black hair covered almost the entire top-half of his face. Nesta recognised the young man immediately as Darren Price, having found him in a similar position on the high street, and was surprised by how much he had chosen to isolate himself even amongst people his own age.

Standing a few yards away from the tree was a group of older teenagers, who were led by a young man called Bevan Charles, an individual that Nesta would recognise anywhere, mainly due to his enormous frame. This giant of a young man was the spitting image of his father, a natural farmer who had also been very big for his age.

Bevan's small entourage gathered around him, as he appeared to be filling up a used *Coke* can with some unpleasant looking liquid. After thrusting the object up into the air like a live grenade, the group watched their creation go flying towards an unsuspecting Darren Price. The impact was enough to send Bevan and his friends bursting into a fit of laughter, as a furious Darren shook out his long hair in the manner of a wet dog after a swim.

The teenager gave the culprits a harsh scowl, before the sound of a loud school bell sent everyone back inside.

Nesta had witnessed the entire scene from the comfort of her window and tutted to herself before walking away.

When she entered the sanctuary of the teacher's lounge, Nesta was surprised to find it almost empty. Standing over by the kettle was a man she had worked with for most of her career. Dewi Pritchard, the school's woodwork teacher, had always made her feel relaxed. His calming nature and laid back approach to life had been a welcome tonic in her small world.

Like many of her colleagues, teaching the town's youth had not been Dewi's first choice of profession either, but the family man had stuck with his first job until the bitter end. Creating objects out of wood had always been a passion of his, anyway, and although he had spent most of his time watching teenagers butcher their materials on a daily basis, it had been enough to keep him satisfied.

"Now there's a sight for sore eyes," said Dewi, holding up his favourite *Everton F.C.* mug (a mug that had lasted in that school as long as he had).

"Dewi Pritchard," said Nesta, who had to restrain herself from hugging the man. "So there *are* some of us left."

Dewi swallowed a mouthful of stale coffee and shook his head. "I thought you managed to escape. What went wrong?"

Nesta smiled. "Someone tempted me back. How could I resist?"

"Let me guess," said Dewi. "Cartrin?" His old friend nodded. "She has a silver tongue, that one. I've got one year left, and then that's it. You won't be finding me back here. I've paid my dues."

"Still saving up for that boat?" Nesta asked.

Dewi shook his head. "Amy's put a stop to that. And she's probably right. We're probably better off with the extension."

"Smart woman." Nesta had known Dewi and his wife since her own school days. She was very fond of Amy but had secretly been jealous on the day they got together during their graduation party. Unlike Amy, she had been too slow and could never resent her for it. "If you do ever get that boat, let me know. I'd quite enjoy a fishing trip on the high seas."

The woodwork teacher chuckled and tried to imagine Nesta having the patience. "Well, they do always say that you're better off knowing a person who owns a boat rather than owning one yourself."

Nesta took another look around the room. "Where is everyone?"

"Hiding, probably," said Dewi. "The morale has been pretty low recently. So many of the old crew have left, and the new blood are not overly social. Then there's the news about Dafydd."

"Yes," said Nesta. "I can imagine that came as quite a shock."

Dewi ummed and ahhed. "You could say that. Although Dafydd was not exactly popular amongst his fellow teachers."

"No?" asked Nesta, genuinely intrigued.

"He had a habit of rubbing a lot of people up the wrong way. The man was a far cry from how I remember him as a lad. He'd started his career teaching in this private school down in the south of England. Proper posh place, apparently. The sort of place famous people sent their children — not that I'd know who any of these famous parents are. You know what I'm like."

Nesta nodded. Her old friend had been a terrible pub quiz partner, especially when it came to popular culture. The fact that he had never heard of Colin Firth still baffled her to this day.

"So you can imagine what it must have been like starting here on the first day," Dewi continued.

"He should have known what it was like," said Nesta. "He attended this school himself." All of a sudden, and despite her reluctance to return for active duty, the teacher was struck with a sudden feeling of defensiveness for her school. Certainly, it was not exactly *Eton College*, but the majority of students came away with very good grades, and the standards were high.

"He had a right stick up his —" Dewi paused and considered his language. "Well, you know what I mean. The man walked around as though he were holier than thou — and thou did not like it one bit."

"Any teachers in particular?" Nesta asked.

Dewi let out a deep breath and tried to think. "Some of the older guard for certain, including myself. I don't care *where* you've taught before, we've all got the same job to do. Young people are the same all across the country: they're insecure, emotional, full of hormones... and it's our job to navigate them as best we can."

"Can you think of anyone who would hate him enough to want him gone?"

The man stared at his old friend with a suspicious smile. "You mean, was there anyone who wanted him —?"

"Yes," said Nesta.

Dewi laughed. "Oh, Nesta. Still got that detective's nose, I see."

"I don't know what you mean."

"Come on," said her old friend. "I remember that time someone ate all the last chocolate biscuits over in that thing." He pointed to a colourful biscuit tin on the kitchen counter. "You practically launched a full-scale investigation!"

Nesta pouted her lower lip in sulk. "I always knew it was Robin Mellon. The greedy sod."

Her fellow teacher scratched his bald head for a moment. "I suppose there was Martin Edwards."

"Arty Marty?" asked Nesta in surprise. She tried to picture the veteran art teacher with his flamboyant shirts, which were always unbuttoned far too low to reveal a glimpse of his hairy chest.

"Martin's been coaching the under-fifteen's rugby team for over a decade," said Dewi. "It's been his pride and joy. They've been top of the league for years. Then, Dafydd Thomas comes waltzing in and insists that he take over.

"Well," said Nesta. "He *is* the sports teacher."

Dewi nodded. "That was exactly Dafydd's point. But all of us know how much rugby means to Martin. He's obsessed. And it was only one team. There's plenty of others that need coaching." The man let out a grave frown. "But Dafydd was just too stubborn. Probably wanted all the glory for himself. They're the best team in the school."

"So it didn't go down well?" Nesta asked.

"Not well at all. Martin's barely been out of his classroom since. He only turns up to mandatory meetings. I think he's put all of his frustrations back into his art. Thank goodness — for Dafydd's sake." The man paused for a moment and remembered what had just happened. He could see the knowing stare coming from his old friend. "Oh, come on, Nesta! Martin might be a little intense, but he wouldn't hurt a fly! The man's a gentle soul at heart."

"I didn't say anything," said Nesta, sipping on her mug of tea.

The silence that followed was suddenly shattered, as the door barged open. Johnny Glyn, the young headteacher, came storming into the room and made his presence known. "Ah! Here you are!"

Nesta looked over at Dewi and knew what he was thinking. They both did a poor job of hiding their discomfort (not that Johnny would ever notice).

"Wonderful to have you back, by the way." The young man grabbed the supply teacher's hand and shook it against her will. "How are you finding it?"

"So far?" Nesta asked. "Invigorating."

"Good, good! That's good to hear. We'll have a proper good chat some other time."

"I shall look forward to it." Nesta took another slurp of her tea, as the stressed headmaster paced around the room in a ball of energy.

"I need to ask you an enormous favour," said Johnny, his overactive mind barely holding its attention.

"I'm listening," said Nesta.

The young man marched back over and gave her a smile so patronising that it was hard to take in what he was about to say.

"Now," said Johnny, bursting with excitement. "How do you feel about physical education?"

CHAPTER 6

The Jack Russell known as Hari went sprinting towards the tranquil lake as though he were on fire. His evening walk was his favourite time of the day (except for his morning walk, breakfast time and dinner time). He struck the water in a blaze of glory, as the reflection of an evening sunset was shattered in a burst of ripples.

Nesta watched her old friend bathing himself in the cold water with a happy smile. It had been a long day, and her return to the world of teaching had been more taxing than when she was full time. Her stamina for educating rowdy teenagers had suffered since retirement, and an evening walk to the lake was just what the doctor ordered.

As she looked out towards the Aran mountain, an unexpected figure kept grabbing her attention. She rarely came across anyone else that time of day and was surprised to see the silhouette of a young man further along the shore. On closer inspection, she discovered that the figure was in fact Darren Price, who appeared to be dashing around with his phone in the air. She also noticed that his chosen spot for this strange activity was also the exact location she had found Dafydd Thomas' body only a few days before.

Darren hadn't even noticed his visitor approaching, until the sight of a small terrier caused him to almost fall over backwards.

"Don't worry," said Nesta, as she saw the wet dog circling the distressed teenager. "He doesn't bite."

"Get him away!" Darren cried, drying his forehead from Hari's splatters of lake water.

Nesta let out a short whistle and summoned her excited dog to come over. "Are you alright?"

Darren breathed a sigh of relief now that Hari had given him some space. "I'm just not comfortable around dogs. They give me the heebies."

"Oh," said Nesta, slightly disappointed. She had always thought Darren was a strange boy; now she was certain of it. "Can I ask what you were doing?"

The teenager seemed annoyed by the question but decided to go ahead and answer anyway. "I'm shooting some content for my channel."

Initially confused, Nesta saw him shake the mobile phone in his hand and assumed he was referring to his online streaming channel (and not BBC 2). The woman took another look at their surroundings which consisted of little more than a lake and some gravel.

"You're covering the wildlife?" she asked.

Darren tried not to groan. "I've found my subject matter — true crime."

"I see," said Nesta. "So, what exactly are you going to cover after this Dafydd Thomas business has died down. Sheep rustling? Trolley thefts? Or what about those people who take the shopping bags without paying for them?"

The teenager ignored her big grin and refused to be

deterred. "I'll cross that bridge when I come to it. First, I'm going to solve this case — and cover the whole thing on my channel."

"Is that right?" Nesta's face brightened, and she decided to take a seat on a nearby picnic table. "Well... how about that, Hari? Looks like we have a real-life Hercule Poirot on our hands."

Darren watched her talking to the Jack Russell and decided that this former teacher was even stranger than he had first thought. "Never heard of that bloke, but whatever."

The young man's comment stunned the supply teacher more than anything that had emerged from his mouth so far. "Excuse me? Are you telling me that you've never heard of Poirot?"

"Sounds like a talking bird," said Darren. He was quite proud of the comparison. Nesta, on the other hand, was downright offended.

"You've really never heard of Agatha Christie?" she asked.

The teenager was quickly losing interest and had already delved into the comfort of his mobile phone screen. "It's some book, right? From almost a hundred years ago by the looks of it..."

Nesta frowned. "Did you just look that up on the internet?"

Darren smiled, as if she had just paid him a compliment. "Who needs books when you've got good-old *Google*?"

The woman opposite him shuddered in disgust. "You must have at least heard of *Murder On The Orient Express*? Everyone knows that one." She saw him reach for the phone again. "Wait! Stop! Don't you dare Goggle it, or I'll set Hari on you!"

He had already grown bored of the conversation and returned to his filming. Nesta watched him with a look of sheer pity. "Dear, dear. You poor thing. Imagine never having had the pleasure of discovering Samuel Ratchett's killer."

An irritated Darren tried to ignore her tutting and kept his focus on the phone. "I bet it was the least obvious person. Probably the butler."

Nesta smiled. "Ah, to be so young and clueless. I envy you in many ways. If I could pay someone to erase my memory of every Agatha Christie book, so that I could enjoy them a second time, I would pay a fortune. You have so much fun in store."

Darren sniggered. "I got no time for sitting around reading. Just give me the film version. Life's too short."

The teacher gasped. The young man might as well have pulled out a dagger and stabbed her straight in the chest. She had never experienced anything so painful since her last dental appointment. "A crying shame," she muttered.

"No offence, like. But I didn't come down here for no English lesson, alright?"

Nesta could see the teenager's frustration and continued to stare at him. "I would say that last sentence was barely English, but I see your point." She stood up and strolled over to where he was standing and looked down at the handful of stones beneath their feet. "So what exactly are you hoping to achieve filming the ground?"

Darren sighed and lifted up his phone to play her the footage. As far as Nesta was concerned, there didn't seem to be anything more than she had already seen.

"I'm starting off at the scene of the crime," he said. "Dafydd's body was found right here."

"I know," said Nesta with a smug grin. "I'm the one who found it."

Her remark surprised the young man. "You *did*?"

Nesta nodded. "I was walking my dog, just like I am now, and there he was. I had the pleasure of calling it in." She realised suddenly how pleased her tone was and tried to remember that a man's life had been taken. Although, she had enjoyed being the one to report it. Looking back at it, her unexpected discovery had been the most exciting thing to have happened all year. It was strange how an encounter with the dead could make a person feel more alive. "You're only partially right, though." She pointed to a patch of gravel that was less than a few feet away. "His body was actually over *there*."

Darren frowned. He thought he had done all of the necessary research, which included scouring the web for relevant news articles, and, now, here was this annoying woman who had the nerve to correct him.

"Why didn't you *tell* me that you found the body?" he asked.

Nesta gave him an innocent smile. "Oh, I'm sorry, Mr Holmes. I hadn't realised that this was *your* case. I don't mean to trample on your toes." She leant towards him and whispered. "You do know who Sherlock Holmes is, don't you?"

"Course I do!" The teenager racked his brains and assumed that she was referring to an insurance advert. "How was the guy positioned?"

The woman stared at him. "Are you really asking me to get down on that cold ground and replicate the body?"

The teenager hadn't thought about that idea and gave her a shrug. "Sure. That would help."

Nesta shook her head and spent the next minute or so lowering herself to the floor. The gravel was indeed cold and slightly wet. She placed her head down against the stones and looked up at the pink sky. She remembered Dafydd's position as though it were yesterday and had struggled to get the image out of her head.

"You realise I'll never be getting up ever again now?" she asked, squirming around in the dirt. Just as she couldn't imagine feeling more uncomfortable, an excited Hari came running over to lick her face. "Hari — no! Get off!"

Darren couldn't help but chuckle at the sight of the wet Jack Russell jumping all over his helpless owner.

Once she had endured the incessant licking and her dog had finally lost interest, Nesta looked up to see that the teenager had started filming. "Hey!" she cried. "Don't you dare take that photograph!"

"I'm not taking a photograph," said Darren. "I'm filming."

Nesta's eyes widened. "You had better not! Or that phone will be going straight to the bottom of that lake."

The teenager sighed and lowered his phone. "Alright, so that was how you found him?"

"Pretty much," said Nesta, checking the positions of her limbs.

"So he can't have drowned," said Darren.

"What makes you say that?"

"Last I checked, you can't drown on dry land. You need water."

Nesta rolled her eyes. "Yes, yes. Alright, smart Alec. What if he had drowned first, and then someone fished him out?"

"Why would they do that if someone wanted to kill him?" Darren asked.

"You have to consider every possibility in a case like this. Nothing can be left to assumption." The formerly retired woman dragged herself up from the ground, and the noises she made in doing so reminded Darren of an old car engine.

"I knew that was a bad idea," said Nesta, wiping off the mud from her favourite cardigan.

"Was there any blood?" Darren asked.

Nesta checked herself and gave him a shake of the head. "Not that I can see. But I'll let you know later."

"I meant on Dafydd…"

"Oh," said Nesta, pausing to bring up that haunting image again. She liked to think that her mind was far more efficient than any smart phone or computer, and it was quite capable of recalling information at will (although, if she were really being honest, her internal processing system had become a little more sluggish as of late. But there was no rush).

Darren stood there and waited for her to reply, as her eyes squinted like a pair of closing shutters.

"I don't recall any blood," she said, eventually.

"Are you sure?"

"Why are you so interested in *blood*?" Nesta asked back. "The man was dead. You teenagers are obsessed with gore and violence from those wretched *Gameboys*."

"*Gameboy*?" Darren smirked. "Who the hell still plays with *Gameboys*?"

"Whatever they're calling it now. Either way, those things will turn your brain into mulch."

"So no blood?"

"No blood!"

The disappointed young man sighed. "That's a shame. It might have given away how he died." He looked over at the patch of gravel where Nesta had just been covering. It was hard to imagine a dead body in such a calm and tranquil location. A graveyard was no different, he supposed, but there was rarely ever an act of violence in a cemetery. Whoever had chosen to end Dafydd's life would have had to get their hands dirty in delivering that fatal blow. The peaceful surroundings didn't exactly encourage hostility.

Darren turned to Nesta and pointed towards his mobile phone. "Would you mind doing an interview?" he asked.

"I beg your pardon?" Nesta asked back.

"For the channel. It would be awesome to include the person who found the body."

"It's completely out of the question," said Nesta.

The budding social media influencer jumped forward and began filming her anyway. "Come on," he said. "You don't need to say much. Just say what you said to me, and tell them you found the body. It'll make everything really legit."

"Absolutely not! There is no chance in a million years that I'm going to allow myself to be immortalised forever on some Ticky-Tocky Faceygram nonsense. You won't find me featuring on something that's watched by people in their underwear. And that's that!"

Moments later, Nesta was tidying up her hair whilst the teenager rolled his phone camera. She wasn't entirely happy with the light on her face, but it would have to do.

"What exactly am I supposed to say?" she asked.

"Whatever you want to say," said Darren, circling her like an obsessed fashion photographer.

The teacher turned to face the phone and stared directly into the camera lens. "Now, you listen up, people of the interweb! Do yourselves a favour and turn this phone off. There's nothing to see here! That's right — I'm talking to *you*, the man with *Dorritos* on his belly. Go out into the world and do something useful. This screen isn't making you happy. It's just slowly killing your soul, a day at a time. Put me down, right now, and slowly walk away. I mean it, people of the phones! You lazy little monkeys! You'll thank me for it later."

Darren ended his recording with a perplexed expression.

"How was that?" asked Nesta.

"Not exactly what I had in mind," said Darren. He watched the woman round up her Jack Russell.

"Right," she said. "I think we're about done here, wouldn't you agree?"

The teenager nodded. He supposed they were.

CHAPTER 7

Aled Parry was sitting in his parked police car with a relieved smile. He had been waiting for this moment all morning. A chance to enjoy his sausage roll from the local butcher's was often a highlight of his working day, and he was determined to savour it as much as possible. As he removed the piping-hot pastry from its packet, the smell of heaven wafted up his nostrils and caused his mouth to water; it was time for the first bite.

Just as the sausage roll was on the verge of making contact with his lips, a loud knock against the driver window caused him to jump in fright. The police officer winced, as the pastry was much hotter than expected and had caused him to burn his tongue.

With a reluctant grunt, Aled wound his window down to reveal the face of Nesta Griffiths.

"Hope I'm not disturbing you," she said.

The police officer looked down at his sausage roll which had now been crushed from the frightened jolt. "I was in the middle of something, actually."

He watched his former sergeant's wife make her way around

the front of the police car before plonking herself down in the seat beside him and closing the door.

Nesta was struck by the smell of sausage roll almost immediately and realised that she was quite peckish herself.

"What is it that I can do for you?" Aled asked, brushing off the crumbs from his lap.

"Now come, Aled. What's a little catch up between friends?"

The police officer gave her a cynical frown. "We only just spoke the other day."

"That reminds me," said Nesta. "How's the Dafydd Thomas case progressing?"

Aled nodded. He knew there was a reason for her visit. "You're asking the wrong person, I'm afraid. The case is being handled by the regional detective sergeant. I'm helping as best as I can, obviously, but nothing more than that."

Nesta nodded. "Of course, of course. That makes sense." She turned to him with a mischievous smile. "Don't tell me you're not curious, though? A strapping, young and ambitious local police officer like yourself. You could probably crack this entire case in a few weeks."

The young man chuckled. "I think you overestimate my abilities, Nesta. I'm very flattered."

"Surely you're dying to at least have a crack at it?" Nesta asked.

Aled shook his head. "I'm afraid there's just not enough hours in the day, sadly. I have very few resources at my disposal and the workload is already piling up."

The woman beside him looked down at the pile of crumbs on his shirt. "Yes, I can see that."

She sat back in her chair and stared out through the grubby windscreen. The high street was quiet and possessed a slight eeriness — the type of eeriness that came when a killer was on the loose. Although, this feeling was probably all in Nesta's head.

"So," she said. "At least we know now that we have a murder on our hands."

Aled glanced at her whilst trying to finish off the rest of his lunch. The thought of murder was not what he wanted midway through a sausage roll. He was also surprised at her use of the word "we". "I had a feeling it was murder. I even told the detective."

Nesta hummed. "Yes, that will be your honed police officer's gut kicking in there." They both ignored the rumbling sound coming from Aled's stomach. Unfortunately, sausage rolls didn't always agree with him. "Do we happen to know the cause of death?" she asked, trying to be as casual as possible.

Aled nodded with his mouth full and waited until he could swallow. "Blow to the head."

The woman beside him nodded. "Interesting… a blunt object, per chance?"

"Most probably," said Aled. "Although that could be anything."

"That blow wasn't caused by collapsing to the floor?" Nesta asked. "He could have blacked out from too much alcohol. Knocked his head on the ground and that was that."

Aled shook his head. "The forensic reports show that he would have been struck in the head before he landed."

"Any ideas how long before?"

The police officer shook his head again. "No idea. Didn't think to ask."

Nesta tried not to look frustrated. She had half a mind to clip the man around the ear, but she didn't fancy being arrested for assault (although an excuse not to attend her next teaching assignment would have been quite welcome).

"Have you spoken to Geraint Owen recently?" she asked.

Aled raised an eyebrow. "Geraint Fedw Las? The farmer? Why, yes, I have, actually. I spoke to him Friday night. I got called out to *Plas Coch* over an assault."

"Involving Dafydd Thomas?" Nesta gave a knowing smile.

"Yes..." The police officer glared at her, suspiciously. He had been so distracted by Dafydd's death that he had almost forgotten about the incident at the pub the night before and hadn't even thought to link them together.

"Have you spoken to him since?"

"No," said Aled. "The charges were dropped. And if you're implying this altercation might be linked to Dafydd's murder, then that's up to the detective. He's aware of the incident."

"Fair enough," said Nesta, without any effort to hide her disappointment. "Why should you? It's not *your* job to get involved."

"No," Aled said again, this time with a stern tone in his voice. He was becoming irritable and had grown tired of the questions, especially on his lunch break. "It's *not* my job. I've got enough to do."

Nesta nodded. "What about Donna Lloyd — Dafydd's fiance? Have you managed to speak to her?"

"No. I haven't *managed*."

"Righto," said Nesta. "Say no more." She could sense the police officer's bad mood and decided not to press the matter any further. "How was your sausage roll?"

Aled gave her a miserable frown. Despite his best efforts, his uniform was still covered in pastry crumbs. "Too hot," he said. "I burnt my tongue."

"Ah, yes. You have to watch that. It depends on who serves you at that shop." She leant towards him and whispered: "Word of advice — give it a few more minutes to cool down. It's the same with the pasties."

She gave the police officer a friendly wink and left the car to leave him in peace.

∼

DONNA LLOYD HAD BEEN SHOPPING at Bala's local supermarket since the days of *Kwik Save*. Despite having changed hands many times since then, the size of the building had not altered one bit. On this particular day, the aisles of food felt smaller and more cramped than usual — at least, it did for Donna Lloyd.

There weren't that many more people than usual (in fact, it was one of the quieter times of the week), and the staff levels were at a minimum, but, for a reason unbeknownst to herself, Donna was feeling extremely overwhelmed by her fellow shoppers. Perhaps it was all in her head, she thought, or maybe it was the fact that everyone kept staring at her.

News travelled fast in that town, and most people knew what had happened to her fiancé.

It was almost as though Donna could read each person's mind as they went past, as though she could hear their incessant whispers, their passing judgement, and, in some cases, their hollow pity. Her paranoia was further increased by the appearance of her mother's friend, who gave a sympathetic nod and began offering her condolences as they stood there in the frozen food section.

"You poor thing, love. We were all shocked. Such a lovely man as well."

The more the woman spoke, the more Donna realised how little this family friend actually knew her deceased partner. It had been the same case for most people she had spoken to since the day he died. How strange it was, she thought to herself, that as soon as a person died, all anyone could ever say about them was positive.

Donna knew full well that her former boyfriend was no saint, but that didn't seem to stop borderline strangers gushing over his memory like a broken record.

By the time she had made it to the baked goods section, Donna had the urge to grab her trolley full of food and charge it straight past the tills and into the high street. After a deep breath, she grabbed the box of eggs from the top shelf and checked it for cracks. As she closed the lid back up and turned to place the container in her trolley, her arm collided with something moving at high speed. In a split second, the eggs had flung from her hand and were now splattered across the polished floor.

"Oh!" a voice cried. "I'm so sorry!"

Standing beside her trolley was a person that Donna used to dread the sight of back in her youth. Not much had changed since then, only this time, the teacher's appearance at least stopped her lashing out with a furious expletive.

"Mrs Griffiths…"

Nesta continued her Oscar-winning performance and danced around the puddle of egg yolk with her best distraught expression.

"I didn't even see you there," said Nesta. "I was in such a rush to get this shop done."

"I know the feeling," said Donna, trying to wipe her gooey toe against the steel trolley leg. "I can't wait to get out of here."

The teacher cupped her mouth and began crying out for help in the manner of a stranded sailor: "Help! We need help, over here! Spillage! Spillage on aisle —" She looked up for a number but found nothing but a banner advertising chicken wings. "Spillage in baked goods! Spillage in baked goods!" Nesta reached out towards the nearby shelf. "Here, let me get you another one."

Donna cringed, as the older woman began rooting through

the remaining egg boxes for her. "No, please... there's really no need."

Her words were ignored, and she was soon handed a fresh box that she wanted to chuck into the air.

"They really need to put these in a safer spot," said Nesta. "I mean, they're asking for trouble putting them here."

"Where exactly do you suggest?" asked Donna. "A chicken coup?"

The teacher howled with laughter. "You always did have that cheeky humour on you. I often struggled to keep a straight face."

Donna's stiff posture loosened. "I suppose I did have a bit of a mouth on me back then. Not much has changed in that regard."

"You were as bright as a button, though." Nesta studied the young woman's tired face. Donna looked as though she'd not slept for an entire week, and her clothes appeared to have been cobbled together for a quick run to the shops. "Do you remember your school reports?"

Her former pupil nodded. "Needs to try harder." Donna sighed. "Maybe if I'd taken your advice back then, I would have done better in university. I just scraped through by the skin of my teeth. You can't really get away with slacking at that level."

Nesta was curious to know exactly what degree classification she had graduated with, but something told her that it had been below expectations, and she decided to leave it. "You went to *University College London*, didn't you?"

Donna nodded.

"The same university as —"

"Yes. The same as him." A sadness washed over Donna's face, as she was struck by the distant memory of their secondary school graduation. "We'd planned it all out. We applied for the same universities so that we could end up in the same location. Amazingly, we both got into UCL, which was a huge stroke of luck at the time. We were over the moon."

"You both really loved each other," said Nesta, thinking back to her own first relationship. She had not spoken to Emyr Wyn in decades but would never forget him. The memory of that first experience, falling head over heels with another person — it never really left a person. Nesta had often wondered what became of Emyr Wyn and hoped that his life had been happy.

"I'd never been with anyone else," said Donna. "Dafydd was my first boyfriend. I was his first girlfriend. It was all we knew. I couldn't imagine us being apart. When we both got into the same university I cried. It was too perfect."

"*Too* perfect?" asked Nesta.

Donna saw the look of concern in her eyes. "Yes, well. Nothing's ever perfect, is it? We were a bit miserable for a few years. After uni, we had grown to enjoy the city life, so we stayed. But Dafydd began to get more and more unhappy. He hated his teaching job. The pay was good, but living in London was so expensive, and we didn't really notice the difference. I was fed up with my jobs, too."

"Jobs?"

"I kept changing where I worked almost every few months," said Donna. "Like I said, my degree was pretty underwhelming. So I got stuck doing office jobs that I could do standing on my head. I was bored out of my skull." She paused, and her eyes darkened. "But Dafydd was even more unhappy than I was. He seemed a bit... lost... or unfulfilled, somehow. Even though the school he was teaching at was a very good one."

"I heard that he was teaching the sons and daughters of famous people," said Nesta.

Donna looked up for a moment after staring at the floor. She seemed surprised at the other woman's knowledge. "Yes, a few of them were. Like I said, it was a good school. He was very lucky to start his career there. But it didn't seem to make him happy." She turned her attention back to the floor. "A few years after starting there, he began to go out a lot. He was drinking more at home, too. His colleagues even started to notice. In the end, the headteacher had to have a conversation with him. That's when we knew things were bad. So, I suggested we move back home to Bala. I was expecting him to shut the whole idea down straight away. But he didn't. If anything, he was all for it, like he had wanted to do that all along."

Nesta smiled. "Home is where the heart is. It's like gravity — it will always pull you back eventually. Not that I would know! I've never left. But I read it somewhere and always liked the simile."

"I guess it was true for us," said Donna. "We thought the move back would be a fresh start — for both of us. I'd planned to re-train as a teacher."

Nesta's face lit up. "Is that right?" She almost felt a slight flutter of pride. "I'm sure you'd make a great one."

Donna nodded in appreciation. "It was all perfectly planned out. Then —" She struggled to hold back the tears. "Well, you know what happened."

The older woman put an arm around her. "Hey, it'll be alright. Just you see. You're strong enough to get through this."

After consoling her for another minute or two, Nesta and her fellow shopper made their way to the checkout. They barely said another word, as the groceries were scanned and packed into their own carrier bags.

Once they had both made it to the front doors, Nesta lifted up her handful of items and was pleased to find that they were light as a feather.

"Do you want a hand carrying that all back to Mawnog Fach?" she asked, pointing to the other woman's three bags. "I could do with the extra walk."

Donna glared at her. "How do you know I'm living in Mawnog Fach?" she asked.

Nesta could see the fury in her eyes and started to regret her careless proposal. "Oh, I don't know. Someone must have mentioned it."

"Have you been following me?" Donna asked, her voice getting louder.

"Heavens — no! Why would you think that?"

The frazzled young woman tried to restrain herself. Her mind was already racing and that same rush of adrenaline she had felt when leaving the house had returned. She pulled her hand away, as Nesta tried to touch it. "Get away from me! You're just like all the other crazies in this town! Leave me alone and mind your own business!"

Donna stormed off and left the teacher completely dumbfounded. Nesta stood in between the automatic doors and could see the people around her all staring. Perhaps Donna was right, she thought to herself. People really *did* need to mind their own business.

CHAPTER 8

It had taken Nesta even longer than usual to make the long walk from the teacher's lounge to the music department. Her mind was still distracted by the awkward ending to her meeting with Donna Lloyd. Although she had indeed taken the opportunity to bump into Dafydd's fiancée on purpose, Nesta had only followed her from the post office to the supermarket (and not from her actual house). Even if she *had* resorted to such a thing, it was a strange accusation to make unless you were on the run from the law.

As she made her way past the school's three language departments (Welsh, English and French), the supply teacher could have sworn people were sniggering as she went past. Nesta began to wonder whether Donna Lloyd's paranoia was contagious, until she passed one pupil who literally pointed at her and giggled.

"Nesta's Natter!" another pupil called out, before he ran away up a flight of stairs towards the science lab. Nesta had a right mind to chase the young man down and hold his hair against a Bunsen burner until he explained himself, but, instead, she noticed an upcoming figure sitting in one of the window alcoves.

"Not hungry?" she asked, checking her watch.

Darren Price turned to look at her and removed his headphones. "Have you *eaten* in that cafeteria?" he asked.

Nesta winced. "Yes, fair point. I did try their famous curly fries once but that was in the late eighties." She waited for the teenager to laugh, but, instead, he merely stared at her. This new generation had no sense of humour, Nesta thought.

Facing the moody teenager, it was difficult not to be distracted by the group of young males in the window behind him. Unbeknownst to Darren, who had his back against the glass, Bevan Charles and his group of friends were dancing around outside like a pack of wild animals. Like Darren, Nesta tried to ignore their wild cries, until Bevan's face slammed against the glass and performed an enormous kiss that disfigured his face.

"Get away!" Nesta cried, running to the side door. The teacher's sudden appearance in the doorway caused the gang to disperse almost immediately, and they scurried away like rowdy pigeons.

She returned to Darren's favourite windowsill and could still see the large stain from Bevan's lips in the glass behind him.

"Friends of yours?" she asked.

Darren scoffed, having yet to turn around. "They're a bunch of nobodys."

"Well, I know one of those nobodys is a *somebody* called Bevan Charles," said Nesta. "The big lump is a chip off the old block."

"He just doesn't like me because I punched him in the face on the first day of school," Darren muttered. Nesta raised an eyebrow and waited for him to elaborate. "He made fun of my Iron Maiden shirt and long hair. So I stuck my fist in his face. He's been calling me *Maiden* ever since."

"Well," said Nesta, slightly taken aback. She quite enjoyed

the thought of Bevan Charles getting what he deserved, but the veteran teacher knew full well that *his* sort could never have the sense knocked out of them. "I can't say I condone violence. What happened after you punched him?"

"He grabbed my hair and we both got detention," said Darren. "He likes to make sure that there's a strong group around him now before he says the word *Maiden* again."

Strength in numbers, Nesta thought. That sounded about right. Some things never changed. "I wouldn't let a numpty like him ruin your enjoyment of school."

Darren chuckled. "Enjoyment? Right, sure. I hate school way more than Bevan Charles."

"You do?" asked Nesta, shocked that anyone could not enjoy the thrills of education. "That's a great shame. I heard you were quite talented."

The teenager looked up at her with a confused frown. "Where did you hear that?"

"Mr Lewis."

Just the mere mention of his maths teacher caused Darren to cringe. He could smell the man's cheap aftershave already. "He was probably being sarcastic. The guy can't stand me."

"I would say that's just his temperament," said Nesta, "I don't think he really likes anyone. But he *did* say that you have a natural gift for algebra." She smirked. "He even said it made him annoyed."

"Annoyed?"

"Well, not everyone is naturally gifted at something. He said he was the lowest performer in university and had to work extra hard to get his maths degree. Apparently, people like you make him a bit sick."

"Mr Lewis was the lowest in his class?" The teenager felt his mouth distort into a wry smile. His maths teacher had always maintained a certain air of superiority when conducting his classes, as though everyone else around him were complete fools. He would never look at the man the same way ever again.

"So count yourself lucky," said Nesta. "Some of us would rather endure torture than wrestle with a mathematics formula — myself included."

The teenager shrugged. "I just see formulas as puzzles."

"You like puzzles?"

"I suppose so," said Darren. "I used to do a lot of them when I was younger. My mam used to buy me these puzzle books. I still do some online when I feel like it."

Nesta nodded. "You remind me of my late husband. He loved anything puzzle-related: crosswords, sudoku, jigsaws... sometimes I used to think he treated his job like a puzzle."

"What was his job?" the teenager asked.

"Police sergeant."

That made a lot of sense, Darren thought. If there was ever a closer profession to being a teacher, it was being a police officer. The similarities were endless: law and order, discipling people, dishing out various punishments which involved a lack of freedom...

"He never had a case like this one," said Nesta, staring out of the window.

The teenager looked up. "You mean, the murder case?" Nesta didn't react and continued her mysterious trail of thought. "It's not that difficult," Darren added. His remark caught the woman's attention again. "Well, it's obvious who did it." The attention on him was growing whilst the teacher waited for his big reveal. "It was his girlfriend."

Nesta was disappointed. "You mean, fiancée?"

"Sure, whatever. Either way, it's always the partner."

"Well," said Nesta. "Thank you for taking the time to solve *that* one. I guess we can officially consider this case closed, Mr

Poirot." She saw the name go straight over his head again, and she sighed. "Which reminds me —"

Darren watched the woman reach into her handbag to pull out a disheveled, old paperback. "You know what else is a puzzle?" she asked him, lifting up the book to reveal a cover featuring a steam train and the title: *Murder On The Orient Express*.

"Seriously?" the teenager asked. "You're going to trick me into reading one of your Parrot books?"

"It's pronounced *Poirot*," she said. "And it's not a trick. Thirteen suspects, one location and one victim. That sounds like a pretty good puzzle to me."

Darren sniggered. "Nice try," he said. "But you're not my English teacher. And if there's no exam, I ain't reading nothing. I would just watch the movie anyway."

"I am not."

"Hey?"

"It's — I am not — not ain't."

The young man went blank, and the woman in front of him let out a deep breath. "You don't read books, you say? How surprising."

Darren frowned. He may not have understood the world of metaphors and alliteration, but he could detect sarcasm when he heard it. "Listen, I'm supposed to be on a lunch break. I don't need no lecture."

Nesta gritted her teeth and restrained herself from correcting him again.

"Besides," Darren continued, "books are on the way out. They're just an old method of processing information. Technology evolves. Like writing letters — now you just make a video call."

The supply teacher felt her temperature rising, and she was just about to give a harsh response, when a group of girls walked past, giggling. She turned around and saw them staring at her like she'd escaped from a zoo.

"Is something funny?" she asked.

One of the young women tried to keep a straight face before saluting her. "We just like to natter, Nesta!"

The teacher was stunned. "I beg your pardon?" She watched them walk away with her jaw dangling wide open.

Nesta turned back to Darren and shook her head. "I'm telling you, these kids today have no respect, whatsoever." She caught a twinkle in the young man's eye and saw that he was trying not to laugh. "What? What is it?"

He pulled out his mobile phone and played her a video. It was footage of her long rant down by the lake, and she saw a number in the bottom left-hand corner. "Seven hundred thousand views?" The video's caption, which was written in large, red letters, filled her with dread: *Nesta's Natter*.

Darren beamed with excitement. "You've gone viral, Mrs Griffiths. Congratulations."

The teacher went pale and tried to process what was happening.

"I uploaded it last night on my channel," he continued. "And the reaction's gone crazy. Look how many likes I've got! People love it!" Darren showed her his screen again, and they gazed down at the enormous figure above a thumbs-up button.

"You never said you were going to put that stupid video on the interweb!" Nesta cried.

"I said it was for my channel," Darren snapped.

"Yes — but — I never imagined in a million years that anyone would *actually* —"

"Watch it?" The young man shook his head. "Oh ye of little faith." He paused. "Wait, was that Shakespeare?"

"No!" Nesta snapped. "It's from another little book that you've probably never heard of."

"Another murder mystery?"

"They call it — *The Bible!*"

There was a long silence. Darren had taken the point. Eventually, his expression brightened, as he prepared his next question: "Hey, did you fancy recording another video?" The woman stared at him in disbelief. "We could make it a regular thing. It would really grow the channel."

She was about to snap at him again, when, somehow, she managed to compose herself. Instead of biting his head off, she shoved the paperback in his hand. "Do yourself a favour and read this. Then come back and ask me about recording another — whatever that thing was!"

The teenager watched her storm off and looked down at the paperback. He lifted it up like he'd been handed an ancient relic and was just glad that it didn't require a new charger.

CHAPTER 9

Whilst climbing the long flight of stairs, it suddenly dawned on Nesta that she had never even stepped foot in the art department of *Bala Secondary School* before. In fact, despite spending her entire career within the same building, there were many corners she had never had the excuse to visit.

Martin Edwards' art room had the smell of her grandfather's workshop, a nostalgic and pleasant smell, even if it was dominated by oil paint and turps. Nesta entered the room and was overwhelmed by an explosion of colour. It was unlike any other room in the entire building, mainly due to the rest of the school's pale walls and characterless decor.

The art department was a place of imagination and wonder, inspiring even the most reluctant of creatives, Nesta included. She had always wanted to take an evening class in sculpture or drawing but, as with many things, Nesta had never got around to it. Buried deep beneath her own artistic soul was a fear that she would make a dog's dinner of everything (and not the kind she would make Hari). Her handwriting was second to none, but the written word carried certain restrictions, something she had very much appreciated; you could only go so wrong with drawing the letter 'F' (provided it was legible).

Therefore, her creative ambitions had been rather small up until this point, but there was always still time.

Nesta could hear the art teacher's grunting before she had even entered the room. Martin had always made irritating noises, particularly when he ate, and seemed to be completely unaware of his unusual habit. Now it seemed that he also made noises whilst he painted, which is what he seemed to be doing when Nesta entered his classroom

To Nesta's great surprise, it turned out that the art department actually consisted of two large rooms and a storeroom. Why some teachers were granted more space than others she did not know, but the former English teacher was certainly very jealous. Her younger-self had to make do with a cramped classroom that was either too cold in the winter or too hot in summer, all whilst Mr Edwards seemed to have his own studio.

The art teacher hadn't noticed his curious visitor and, with his back still facing her, he continued brushing away at his giant canvas.

Nesta studied the painting with a confused face. These strokes of colour didn't seem to resemble anything from the real world, and it reminded her of when Hari once coughed up his entire dinner. There were reds and browns and pinks, all melded together in a giant spiral. The whole thing made the English teacher very disoriented, and, if she stared at it long enough, she was in grave danger of revisiting her own last meal.

"Oh!" the man in the loose shirt cried out. "I didn't even hear you come in, Nesta."

His fellow teacher wanted to point out that it was hard to hear *anything* over that insistent grunting, but she knew that old habits died hard.

"I didn't mean to interrupt," she said.

The man glared at her with his wild eyes, which almost popped out a little whenever he got emotional. Martin had an intensity about him that never seemed to die down, and Nesta often worried about his blood pressure. She appreciated that art required a certain degree of passion and emotion, but Martin Edwards always seemed on the verge of a nervous breakdown.

"What do you think?" he asked, pointing to his latest masterpiece.

Nesta took her time with the feedback and tried to think of something positive. "It's very... interesting." All of a sudden, her usual vocabulary had run for the hills and left her flailing around in a state of panic. Fortunately, Martin didn't seem to be bothered by the lackluster response and continued to admire his work with the temperament of a proud parent.

"I call it — Fury!"

He turned to his perplexed visitor with an excited grin.

"Oh," said Nesta. "Uh, yes, I suppose it does resemble the outcome of an angry person."

"It's important to express the moment," said Martin. "You need to follow your instincts. These things can't be pre-planned."

Nesta nodded, as though she perfectly understood. "Well, you've certainly expressed... something."

The art teacher sighed. "It's my therapy, painting. Sometimes I just get the urge to paint. Don't you?"

"Oh, absolutely." Nesta continued to stare at the explosion of colour. "Why, only the other day, I had a sudden urge to paint the bathroom. Didn't happen, though."

"You have to grab these opportunities whilst you can," said Martin, grabbing himself a cloth and wiping down his hands. "It's not often I get this room to myself, but when I do, it's my happy place."

"I'm glad to see that you are happy, Martin. You deserve it. How's Linda, by the way? Keeping well, I hope."

The man's face darkened. "We're not together anymore, actually. The divorce went through in the spring."

"Oh," said Nesta. "I'm sorry to hear that."

There was a short silence, and the supply teacher prayed for a grunt or two.

Suddenly, the art teacher sprang into life again and grabbed his stained coffee mug from the table. "Onwards and upwards, though, eh? Got to stay positive!" He let out one of his manic laughs. "Each new day is like a blank canvas!"

Nesta smiled at him. "Couldn't have said it better myself."

"So," said Martin. "What brings you over to this dark and dingy side of the building?"

Nesta began wandering around the room, admiring the various works of art on display that she presumed were made by the pupils. The sight of a table full of lino prints took her right back to her own school days, where she accidentally cut her finger whilst carving out her own print. She glanced at her hand and saw that the scar was still there.

"Nothing much," she said. "Just thought I'd say a quick hello now that I'm back. It's been a while."

The art teacher appeared to be quite touched. People didn't usually come and visit him. If anything, he could have sworn that many of them downright avoided him. "Glad to have you back," he said with a toast of his cold instant coffee.

"Are you still coaching rugby?"

Nesta's question caused the man to almost choke on his drink.

"Yes," he said, his jovial mood soured. "I imagine you've heard the news."

"Absolutely," said Nesta, feigning an innocence that didn't really suit her. "I hear the under-fifteens team are doing well."

Martin gave her a suspicious squint. "I was talking about Dafydd Thomas..."

"Oh!" The woman placed an embarrassed hand over her mouth. "I'm sorry, yes. Terrible thing that happened. And so young."

"Quite," said Martin with another slurp of his coffee. "If you must know, the under-fifteens team is in a diabolical state."

"Really?" asked Nesta, genuinely surprised this time.

The art teacher placed his mug down and wandered back over to the canvas. He stared into his great masterpiece as though the spiral of paint was hypnotising him. "That team was my pride and joy. They were a shambles when I first started coaching them: they couldn't tackle, couldn't pass and half of them didn't even know what a scrum was. With a lot of time and patience we addressed all of their issues, and they suddenly started winning."

Nesta listened with great fascination. She had never been very interested in rugby — or any sport for that matter — but could still appreciate the journey of a group of people striving to be the best. It was the classic foundation of many literary works and a story that had stood the test of time. Rugby matches in Bala were the modern equivalent of two Greek Gods, battling it out in a great arena. She still preferred snooker, of course, but could see the appeal.

"It sounds like they were lucky to have you," she said.

"You can say that again," said Martin with a frustration in his voice. "I watched them go from the bottom of the league to the top — I devoted hours of my spare time to make sure that they were ready for each game. And then what happens?" He turned around to face her, his wide eyes almost bloodshot. "That arrogant idiot arrives and decides he's better qualified."

"I assume you're talking about Dafydd," said Nesta. He

grunted in response, which she took as a "yes". "He started coaching the team himself?"

The art teacher grimaced and headed over to the window, which also happened to look out towards the playing fields. "I even offered to help out as an assistant coach. Can you believe how hard that was? And, still, he rejected the idea. Said it would be a distraction for the players. So, I left him to it." He continued to stare at the goal posts in the distance. "And what happened? Within a week, the team started losing. That was it, then. Their confidence was shattered. They started losing again and again, like some god-awful streak they couldn't get out of. It's like he jinxed them. That man was a curse!"

"I didn't realise that you were so superstitious," said Nesta.

"Every sportsperson is a little," said Martin. "It comes with the territory. I used to wear the same pair of socks for every game in my youth. It was a ritual."

Nesta hoped that these socks he was referring to had at least been washed. "I suppose I never walk under a ladder if I see one," she said. "And I'm always a little disheartened if I see just one magpie. But I don't mind black cats." The man didn't seem to be listening and was still lost in his own angry thoughts. "Do you really think Dafydd could have cursed the under-fifteens rugby team, though, Martin?"

"Well," said the art teacher. "They still haven't won a game since. I've returned as their coach now that Dafydd has — well, you know, gone. But our game last night was shocking. They're a far cry from the young men I knew before he took over. I don't know if they'll ever recover."

His fellow teacher wandered over to a painting on a nearby wall. She was fairly certain that it was a Monet, but her art history was a little hazy (and, judging by the peeling corners, she was fairly certain that it wasn't an original). "I'm sure, if anyone can whip them back into shape, it's you, Martin."

Her compliment loosened the art teacher's tight shoulders, and he took a deep breath to calm himself down. "Yes, we'll get there."

"Tell me," said Nesta. "Did anyone else you know have a bone to pick with Dafydd Thomas?"

Martin turned around with a frown. "Excuse me?"

"Are there any other teachers that you know of who might have harboured a similar resentment to the man? He didn't seem to play very well with others."

The art teacher's shoulders began to tighten again. "What exactly are you suggesting?"

"I'm not suggesting anything —"

"Is this what you've come here for?" Martin snapped. "To fish for gossip and start rumours?"

"Not at all," said Nesta, raising up her arms in a bid to de-escalate the situation. "Please, Martin, you need to relax. It sounds like you might be under a lot of stress."

"I'm not stressed!" the man yelled out. There was a pause, and he seemed embarrassed about his sudden outburst. He closed his eyes and tried to remember his mindfulness training. Deep breaths, he thought. "Dafydd Thomas was an unpopular man. There are plenty of others who would say the same."

"Any people in particular?" Nesta asked. She knew she was pushing her luck, but there was no harm in asking.

Martin grinded his teeth and tried to remember what his mindfulness teacher had taught him: three seconds in through the nose and three seconds out through the mouth. "If you really want to speak with someone who hated his guts, I would give Huw Caradog a try."

"The caretaker?" Nesta asked. "He's still around?" She could still picture the tall man in his long trench coat, roaming the school corridors like a dark shadow. Huw had always kept to himself, and Nesta had only ever exchanged brief pleasantries with the man. She couldn't fathom how someone could have such beef with a gentle soul like Huw Caradog. He would always smile as he went past and didn't seem to have a bad word to say about anyone.

"Dafydd did not like that man one bit," said Martin. "And, as far as I'm aware, the feeling was mutual."

"I see," said Nesta. "Well, I won't keep anymore of your time." Having outstayed her welcome, she had no desire to stay in the man's company any longer than she had to. "Good luck with finishing the rest of the painting," she said, turning to face his canvas.

The art teacher clenched his jaw and glared at her. "I think you'll find that it's already finished…"

"Oh," said Nesta, and she let out a nervous laugh. "Why, so it is! It must be the new prescription glasses. My eyesight isn't what it used to be…"

CHAPTER 10

Huw Caradog stared at the broken window with the pain of a man with a broken heart. The shards of smashed glass were *his* problem now, and he knew, deep down, that the culprit behind this mess would never be brought to justice. As he kissed goodbye to the next thirty minutes of his life, the giant of a man could sense a presence nearby.

"Oh, it's you, Nesta."

Easily at the age of retirement himself, Huw still possessed an enormous frame and his great height meant that he dwarfed most people that came into contact with him. Sometimes, he regretted not taking the rugby a little more seriously in his youth and perhaps could have lifted up a trophy or two instead of pieces of shattered glass.

"I didn't see you," he said with his deep voice.

Nesta had most certainly seen *him*, and, even with *her* eyesight, it was impossible not to spot Huw Caradog from a distance. She looked up at him like a curious hobbit and smiled.

"People have no respect for school property," she said.

The caretaker chuckled. "You can say *that* again. It's the second time this year."

"I'm surprised you're still here, Huw."

The man checked his watch. "Yes, I suppose it is a bit late. But I can't leave all this overnight."

"I meant," said Nesta, "I'm surprised you haven't retired."

Huw burst out laughing and scratched the stubble on his round chin. "Yes, I suppose I'm a bit late doing that, too. Knowing me, I'd only get bored. There's still a couple of years left in me yet. So, tell me, what does retirement actually feel like?"

Nesta pondered his question. She hadn't really thought about it. The weeks and months since she had retired had somehow managed to fly by. It was funny how even the simplest of daily routines could occupy a person's time: walking the dog, cleaning the house, doing the shopping, returning the library books... pretty soon, there wasn't much of the day left, and she had begun to wonder how she'd managed to fit in a full time job in the first place. The numbers on the clock hadn't changed, and, yet, still, the hours had passed. She supposed that time was essentially just down to personal interpretation.

"Retirement feels... very uneventful."

Huw cackled. "I knew it! Like I said — boring! Nah, you can keep your retirement nonsense. I'll retire when I'm dead." He picked up his brush and began sweeping up the broken glass with a chirpy whistle.

"Am I right in thinking that you never got married?" Nesta asked.

"That's something else I never quite got around to doing," said the caretaker. "Probably just as well. I'm an absolute nightmare to live with. And you wouldn't want to share a bed with legs as long as mine. Trust me. There's not a duvet long enough." He laughed again. "It's funny to think that there's a woman out there who could have ended up being my wife. That lucky woman! Talk about dodging a bullet!"

"I wouldn't sell yourself so short, Huw."

"Short?!" The man gave her a mischievous grin. "Who are you calling short?"

They both chuckled this time.

"Alright," said Nesta. "Poor choice of words. You never would have thought I was an English teacher."

"How about you?" asked Huw, as he continued sweeping. "Any men on the horizon?"

Nesta looked back at him in shock. His question had completely thrown her. "Who said I was even looking?" She couldn't help but blush and knew that the caretaker had noticed.

"Don't sell yourself so short, remember? I have the utmost respect for Morgan Griffiths, God rest his soul, but you're back on the market now."

"Oh, stop it!" Nesta folded up her arms in a sulk. "I'm not a sheep."

Huw took a moment to rest his body and leant against the brush handle. "There we have it. Looks like we're both destined to live out the rest of our lives alone."

"Sounds good to me," said Nesta. "At least an empty pillow doesn't snore."

The man laughed. "I hope the rest of your retirement turns out to be more eventful for you, Nesta."

"Speaking of eventful..." The teacher looked down the corridor to make sure that they were still alone. "What do you make of that Dafydd Thomas business?"

The mere mention of the former sports teacher's name clearly made the caretaker uncomfortable. "What about it?" He lifted up his brush and went back to sweeping. The harsh sound of broken glass being dragged around the floor filled the air for a moment.

"It's been quite a shock for everyone," said Nesta.

Huw scoffed, a reaction that surprised the teacher. "Shock," he said. "That's *one* word for it."

"Do you have another?"

"How about — relief?" The man stopped brushing and saw the judgemental frown. "Listen, I feel for his family and all of that, but I'm not going to cry any tears over the bloke."

"Something tells me that you both didn't quite see eye to eye…"

"You reckon?" For the first time since Nesta had known him, this so-called 'gentle giant' exposed an emotional side to him. "The man almost got me sacked. Twice!"

"He did?"

The caretaker squeezed the broom handle with his enormous hands. "I once caught him bunking off school when he was a lad. I was down by the post office and I saw him coming out of *Derwen's*." He pictured the teenager standing in the doorway of the local shop, clutching his bag of sweets. "We both stared at each other. There was nothing to be said. He knew he'd been caught. I assumed that would be enough to prevent him from doing it again, but the next time, I caught him grabbing a burger from the kebab shop. So, I decided to confront him. I told Dafydd that, if I caught him again, I'd report it to the school headteacher. He almost seemed amused, like he had no respect whatsoever." Huw's face conveyed an anger that made Nesta quite concerned about the broom. The handle could only take so much pressure, and the man's grip seemed to tighten with every second. "The third time," he continued, "I'd had enough. There he was, walking down Arenig Street as if he didn't have a care in the world. I told him that was it — I had no choice but to report him. And he just laughed and went on to insult me."

"What kind of things did he say?" Nesta asked. She could feel the caretaker's frustration. If a pupil had treated her with such disrespect, she would have given him a right earful.

"The usual things," said Huw. "I'm no stranger to the taunts of unruly teenagers. I've been in this job for a long time. Although, normally, it's childish calls from a distance. I hardly blend into the scenery." He paused to remember his moment in the side street. "But this was different. The lad was right in front of me. He started ridiculing my job, saying I was nothing but a glorified cleaner and that I should be embarrassed. I didn't take any notice, of course, but then he threatened me."

"Threatened you?"

"He said, if I reported him to anyone, he would tell everyone that I hit him." Huw's breathing increased in speed. "He said he'd get me sacked. I was fuming..." The man's voice started to break and went from anger to despair. "I wish I'd never done it, but it happened so quickly. I was so cross!"

Nesta took a deep breath. "What did you do, Huw?"

The caretaker began to get teary. "I slapped him straight across the face!"

"I see," said Nesta.

Huw wiped his eyes and cleared his throat. "I'm not proud of it! If anything, I'm downright ashamed. I've never hit anyone in my life. But something in the way that boy spoke to me just triggered something." He took a deep breath and began to feel as if a weight had been lifted. Huw had never told anyone this story, and, despite the painful memory, it felt good to get it off his huge chest. "I suppose, if he was going to report me for hitting him, I might as well have done it anyway." He let out a nervous laugh but saw that the teacher wasn't laughing with him.

"What happened next?" she asked.

"That was the strangest thing," said Huw. "He never reported it. Don't get me wrong, he was shocked after I hit him, and he gave me the dirtiest look afterwards. I was probably more shocked than he was, and I think he knew it. He went on to give me this smile, like he knew he'd broken me. But he said nothing, and we just parted ways. That was the end of it. I never saw him skipping school again."

"Sounds like you knocked some sense into him," said Nesta. "Not that I ever condone violence in any form."

"You would think so," said the caretaker. "But I don't think he ever forgot it."

"What makes you say that?"

"Well, many years later, when Dafydd came back to our school as a teacher, he acted like he had some kind of vendetta against me." The man scratched his bald head and sighed. "I tried to make an effort on his first day — you know, welcomed him aboard and all that. But he seemed so… cold." Huw shuddered. "He gave me that same look he gave me in the side street all those years ago. I never forgot it." His expression turned angry again. "Next thing I know, he's spreading rumours that I'm not doing my job properly — that I'm skiving — me! Of all people — *skiving*!" The broom handle began to receive his wrath again, and Nesta was certain it was going to snap. "One day, I got called into the head teacher's office — like some naughty schoolboy! Apparently, someone had reported that they'd seen me down the pub, drinking whilst on duty. Well, I knew exactly who that was. Then I had to sit there, listening to a guy half my age dish out a verbal warning for something I didn't even do!"

Nesta waited for the flustered man to catch his breath. "That must have been very hard," she said.

Huw nodded and was on the verge of sobbing. "These baseless accusations kept coming. And there was nothing I could do to stop them."

"Are you sure it was all Dafydd?" asked Nesta.

"Without a doubt," said Huw. "You know why? Because the

day he — the day he was found by that lake was when it all stopped. There haven't been any complaints since. Now, I'm not one to wish death upon anybody." He turned to face his colleague, and his bushy eyebrows shot up to reveal a pair of wide eyes. "But that man had it out for me. And, if I'm truthful, I'm *glad* he's gone."

The teacher had nothing to say in return, which was unlike her. Instead of responding, she nodded her head and turned around to leave.

"Nesta?"

She turned around to see Huw's concerned face. "You won't tell anyone about the slap, will you?"

Nesta showed no expression. "Don't worry. I'm not a person who tends to involve myself in matters that are none of my business."

CHAPTER 11

Nesta's little *Citroën* had seen better days, and, much like its owner, had not been out on the road as much as it would have liked over the last few years.

"Cars love to be used," her late husband had always said. If *that* was true, then Nesta's little car did not like her very much at all. Living and working in the town had meant that she rarely needed to drive anywhere, and, after several flat batteries over the years, she was beginning to take the hint that even the *Citroën* needed to stretch its legs every once and a while.

Fortunately, that Thursday afternoon was the car's lucky day, as Nesta had decided to take it on a little drive towards Fedw Las Farm. The road leading out of Bala was (like most roads) a very steep one, and the old car was groaning for the entire journey.

"You can do it," Nesta whispered, as they left the main road to join a track so bumpy that it caused the inexperienced driver to bob up and down like a jackhammer. The teacher had never seen a route so riddled with potholes in her entire life and was beginning to wonder whether they would ever make it back in one piece.

The view was spectacular but was also rather spoilt by the

series of scraping noises from underneath the car. Every now and again, Nesta peered out of her driver window to catch a glimpse of the town down below which reminded her of a model village she had once seen on her honeymoon. The lake stretched out into the distance and was now a giant puddle surrounded by great mounds of earth on either side.

But there was no time for sightseeing, as she pressed forward whilst whispering sweet nothings into her steering wheel.

She turned another corner and was soon faced with a large, rusted gate. Nesta prayed that this was not going to be the first of *many* obstacles on her journey, and she was soon to be very disappointed. After opening up her third and final gate, the teacher's poor choice of footwear caused her to stumble to her knees into a muddy bank, and she uttered some of the foulest language since giving birth.

The sight of Fedw Las Farm was like a roaring fire on a cold winter's day, and she had never been so pleased to see a tractor in her life. Her little *Citroën* crawled its way into the yard with a final croak, until she put the car out of its misery and killed the engine.

What she hadn't considered until now was the dreadful possibility that Geraint Owen might not have been home. There was not a hope in hell that she would attempt this excursion again and would have been quite happy to camp overnight if she had to. Fortunately for her, she didn't have to wait long, and Nesta was approached by a suspicious young farmer in a flat cap and wellington boots.

Geraint tapped on the car driver window and waited for it to wind down. If he was going to have to redirect just one more lost delivery driver, he was going to explode.

"Can I help you?" he asked. The grubby window slid down to reveal a familiar face, and the last person he had expected to pay him a visit. "Mrs Griffiths?"

"Hello, Geraint." Nesta smiled and wiped away some excess mud from her chin. "I hope it's a good time."

The farmer stared at his former English teacher and looked up at the afternoon sun. "Uh, it's not great timing, actually. I've got errands to run."

"I won't be long," said Nesta.

"Is this about Mabon?" asked Geraint.

The teacher hesitated at the mention of his son's name. "Mabon, uh, well..."

"You'd better come inside." The farmer checked his watch, and, before she could respond, he was already making his way back towards the farmhouse.

Nesta ignored the guilty voice in her head and followed him across the yard.

They entered the house through a thick front door that screeched across terracotta tiles as it opened. The smell of a burning AGA cooker filled Nesta with a warm nostalgia from her youth, as did the act of kicking off her shoes beside a line of wellington boots.

"Do you need a paned?" Geraint asked, firing up the kettle.

"Yes," said Nesta. "A tea — milk, no sugar — would be exactly what I need."

She looked around the room, which served as both a kitchen and a dining room. A plastic highchair still had the remains of a previous meal and toys were scattered across the tiled floor.

"You must have your hands full at the moment."

Geraint turned around and saw her pointing at the highchair. "Oh, yeah. It's an absolute madhouse. I've given up trying to clean. It never lasts more than an hour."

"How old is the little one?" Nesta asked.

"She'll be two in January," said Geraint, pouring the teas. "Sara's taken her out for the afternoon." The farmer finished making the drinks and placed Nesta's mug down in front of her. "Alright, so what's he done, then?"

The teacher was taken aback by his abrupt tone. He seemed tired and moody, but it was difficult to tell whether this was just a bad day at the farm or his usual demeanour. Judging by his antics at the local pub, Nesta assumed it was probably the latter.

"What's *who* done?" she asked.

"Mabon," said the farmer. "That's why you're here, isn't it? If he's disrupting the classes, I'll give him a right hiding."

"Oh, no! It's nothing like that." Nesta clutched her hot mug for comfort. She was starting to think that this trip had been a bad idea. Just as she was about to respond, the phone on the kitchen counter burst into life.

Geraint groaned and headed over to answer it.

"Yes? Oh, sorry, babe. I thought it was that caller again. Yeah, chicken nuggets sounds fine. Don't worry about me. I got pool with the lads down at *The Goat*, remember? Yeah, okay. See you in a bit." Geraint silenced the phone and went back to sit opposite his guest. "I keep getting these calls from people trying to sell me stuff. Does my head in."

"That was Sara?" asked Nesta.

The farmer nodded. "She's just grabbing some things from town."

"How is she these days?" Nesta remembered his wife as a very pleasant pupil to have in her class. How she ended up with the likes of Geraint Owen she would never know.

"Alright, I suppose." The farmer slurped his drink. "She's a good mam."

The teacher nodded. "I didn't realise that you were a member of the pool club."

Geraint raised his eyebrow. "I didn't realise that you were so interested. It's hardly exclusive."

"My Morgan used to be a regular," said Nesta.

The farmer grinned. "Morgan? Morgan Bobby? He was your husband?" The woman in front of him nodded. "I had no idea! Christ, this really *is* a small town." The topic of pool had lightened his mood. "I love a bit of pool, I do. Helps me to relax a bit. A chance to catch up with the lads."

"Oh," said Nesta, flexing her acting chops again. "That reminds me — you used to be friends with that Dafydd Thomas, didn't you?"

The farmer frowned. "We used to hang out back in the day, sure. Until he decided he was too good for this place."

"*This* place?"

"For me, for Emrys, for Jack... for Bala!" Geraint shook his head in disgust. "He went and sodded off to London, didn't he? Fancied himself a bit of a gentleman. Then came crawling back in the end. Over ten years later!"

Nesta blew on her hot tea. She had already expected this point of view after speaking to Sioned at the pub and was keen to delve a little deeper. The teacher reminded herself of a fisherman, waiting, patiently, as her float bobbed around in the water. "So it wasn't much of a school reunion, then?"

Geraint scoffed. "He didn't even tell me he was back. I had to find out at parents' night at the school. You can imagine my surprise when I walked up to the sports teacher desk and found Dafydd sitting there. Dafydd Thomas teaching my own son sports! Talk about a joke."

"I seem to remember you both getting along quite well," said Nesta.

"People change." Geraint stared into his mug and snarled. "And he certainly did. That was the most awkward conversation I'd ever had."

"And that's the only time you ever saw him?"

"He started coaching the under-fifteens," said the farmer. "I used to have to see him when I took Mabon to training and then at the games. We had a few tense moments."

Nesta noticed his fist clench. "*Tense*?"

"Dafydd can't play rugby. I went to school with him, remember? I know how shocking his ball skills are. It would drive me nuts watching him coach. It was even worse at the games." He let out a proud grin. "I'm quite a vocal spectator, actually. I can get riled up at times."

"Can you really?" asked Nesta, the sarcasm in her voice was as clear as the sky through the window. "That's surprising. I had you down as a very mellow type."

Geraint chuckled. "Yeah, well. It's only cause I'm passionate. Those kids need a good dressing down sometimes."

"And how did Dafydd feel about that?"

"We had a few heated arguments on the sidelines," said the farmer. He reflected on the moments of confrontation with a slight degree of pleasure. "I'm not one to hide my opinion. There was one time we nearly got into a fist fight at half-time, but people broke us apart." His smug grin soon flipped the opposite way. "The next thing I know, Mabon was on the bench for the rest of the game. And he stayed there all season. I was livid." He turned his head and looked out the window. The garden outside overlooked a series of green fields which stretched out for miles. Propped up in the corner of the garden was a steel exercise frame with rugby balls dotted around the grass. "I trained that lad of mine hard last year. Every night we went out to boost his fitness and work on his skills."

"Sounds like you push Mabon hard," said Nesta.

"He's got the talent," Geraint snapped. "Like I had. He just needed the discipline. I couldn't believe Dafydd was making Mabon suffer just so he could have a dig at me."

"Is that when you punched him in the pub?"

The farmer's head snapped back to face her. "How did you know about that?"

Nesta shrugged. "Word gets around when there's a bit of action in town."

Geraint stared at her, suspiciously. "He had it coming. I went over to reason with him when I saw him sitting alone. I swallowed my pride and was prepared to be the bigger man — for Mabon's sake. It wasn't easy, and Daf seemed to be enjoying every minute of it. The guy was steaming drunk which didn't help. Then things got heated, and I decked him one. Always good to get the first one in."

"Quite," said Nesta, swallowing the rest of her tea in one gulp. "Well, I think we've covered enough for today."

The gobsmacked farmer watched the woman stand up to grab her coat. "*Hey*?"

"I've taken up enough of your valuable time."

Geraint jumped up and followed her to the door. "But what about Mabon?!"

Nesta turned around and smiled. "Oh, I never said I was here to discuss your son."

"But —"

"I think you might have assumed that." She buttoned up her coat. "And you know what they say about assuming..."

The man went a bright shade of red and looked like he was about to explode. "You can't just —"

"Thank you for inviting me in for the tea," Nesta said. "You see, I'm trying to get to the bottom of this whole Dafydd Thomas business. *Somebody* in this town has to, and, as luck would have it, I've got plenty of time on my hands." Her smile stretched out across the bottom half of her face. "Retirement is such a wonderful thing. Who knew?"

The farmer's head had reached boiling point, and he was so

cross that he couldn't speak. "Who on earth do you think you are?"

The retired teacher turned back around briefly before heading out through the front door. "Who am I?" she asked with a mischievous twinkle in her eye. "Why, I'm Nesta Griffiths!"

CHAPTER 12

Catrin Jones' house was as immaculate as Nesta would have expected. The deputy head teacher had always been organised and smartly dressed since she was a trainee, and her terraced home on the outskirts of Bala reflected her personality perfectly: neat, warm and as transparent as the gleaming windows overlooking her back garden.

"I see the extension is all go," said Nesta, sitting at the kitchen table and gazing at the piles of raw materials outside.

Catrin placed a plate full of cakes in front of her and did a happy little jiggle. "I've always wanted a conservatory. Keith and I decided there's no time like the present."

Nesta sipped her tea with an understanding nod. "The present is all we have. The past is gone, and you can never guarantee the future."

The younger woman gave her friend a confused look. "Are you alright, Nesta? I've never heard you say anything so zen in my life."

"I've been thinking a lot about mortality recently," said Nesta. "Not mine, necessarily. I came to terms with *that* a long time ago. But other people's, the way everyone comes and goes... I suppose nothing ever really stays the same."

"I think you've stayed *exactly* the same," said Catrin with a laugh. "And so has this town. The only thing that changes in Bala is the supermarket chain."

"I wouldn't be so sure about that." The older woman had a distant gaze and a sadness in her eyes. "The bricks and mortar might look the same but the faces change. You'll know what I mean when you get older." She took another sip of tea and saw the fellow teacher staring. "Sorry. I'm in a funny mood. It would have been Morgan's birthday today. I thought it would get easier as the years pass, but it never does."

Catrin placed a hand on hers. "I'm sorry, Nesta." They sat in silence for a moment, until she picked up a cake and raised it for a toast. "To Morgan! Happy Birthday..."

Nesta smiled. "Happy Birthday, Morgan." She bit into the cupcake and felt the cream explode around her mouth. "Mmmh... these are to die for." The supply teacher looked up to see Catrin's morbid expression at her choice of words, and they both burst into laughter.

"So," said the deputy head. "How are you finding it being back at school?"

"Different," said Nesta. "And, yet, the same. It's very strange."

"I hope the pupils aren't giving you a hard time," said Catrin. "I know they can be difficult with supply teachers."

"I'm not your usual supply teacher." Nesta smiled and took another bite of cake. "I can still handle it. Don't you worry about that. Teenagers don't change, at least."

"I don't know. There's the added world of social media and the internet to deal with now. It's an absolute minefield."

"Ah, yes." Nesta rolled her eyes. "I've been very much acquainted with that side of things. But there's always *some* form of distraction when it comes to young people. Back in my day, we had all sorts of new inventions to contend with: video game consoles, provocative pop music, *Sky* television, *MTV*... the list goes on. This Ticky-Tocky business is no different. Teenagers are impressionable, sensitive creatures. Always have been, always will be."

"Which reminds me," said Catrin, who suddenly became very awkward. She stared down at her drink and struggled to maintain eye contact. "There's something I wanted to talk to you about..."

Nesta studied her face and frowned. "What is it?" She waited for the response. "Come on, girl, spit it out."

Catrin began fidgeting with her nails, something she always did when she was anxious. "I've been trying to work out how to tell you this, but... we've received some complaints."

The older teacher's eyes widened. "*Complaints*? About who?"

The deputy headteacher coughed into her hand. "About you, Nesta."

"About — *me*?"

Catrin nodded. "I feel terrible. I'm the one who dragged you back, and now I'm forced to have this awkward conversation."

Nesta showed little emotion, but, on the inside, she was seething. "Did that numpty, John Glyn, put you up to this? Couldn't have the decency to speak to me himself? Get his *own* hands dirty?"

"John will be having his own meeting with you," said Catrin. "He's fully aware of the situation."

"Is that what this is?" Nesta asked, lifting up another half-eaten cake and pointing around the room. "A work meeting?"

"What? No!" The deputy head scrunched her own forehead and created a line of wrinkles. "I invited you here as a friend. And I'm telling you all this — as a friend. I thought you'd want a heads-up before you find out, officially."

Nesta stared at her whilst munching away on her second cake. "Who was it?"

"Hmh?"

"Who made the complaint?"

Catrin sighed. "You know I can't tell you that."

The older woman threw her arms in the air and groaned. "Oh! I see. So you can't tell me as a friend?"

"It's confidential, Nesta. I can't tell anyone."

"Fine," said Nesta, folding up her arms. "I don't need you to tell me. I can work it out for myself."

"Oh, come on." Catrin shook her head and regretted spoiling a nice afternoon tea. "Don't be like this. I wish I never said anything now."

"Was it Dilwyn History? Because I made a joke about his hair transplant? I bet it was, the little weasel!"

"No!" the younger woman snapped. "I never said it was a teacher."

Nesta gave it some more thought. "Martin? Martin 'Arty Pants' Edwards?"

Catrin paused.

"Ah-ha! I knew it!" The supply teacher bashed her fist against the table. "That little snitch... wait until I get a hold of his brushes..."

"You can't go around interrogating people like a private detective," said Catrin. "You're upsetting people."

The other woman was speechless. "In — well, I —"

The host held her stern gaze. "I know what you're up to. I could see it in your eyes at the chip shop. You think you can solve Dafydd's murder?"

"How dare —" Nesta paused and sighed. "There's no harm in asking a few questions."

"There is when you rock up at people's houses!"

Catrin's harsh words surprised her friend. Another penny

had dropped, and Nesta knew exactly what she was referring to. Perhaps the visit to the farm had been a step too far, but she knew full well that, given the choice, she would have probably done it again.

"Geraint Owen?" she asked in a sulk. "That moody man called the school?"

The deputy head sighed. "What did you think was going to happen? He's the parent to one of our pupils."

"He's a little toerag is what he is. I've known him since he was a lad, and he was trouble even back then."

"But now he's a father," said Catrin. "And we have to respect that."

Nesta nodded and folded up her arms in protest. She knew her friend was right, but that didn't mean she had to like it.

"Anything else I've done?" she asked.

Catrin let out another awkward cough and tried to keep a straight face. "Actually, there was this one other thing…" Whilst the older woman's blood pressure started to rise again, she reached for her mobile phone and searched through the icons on her screen.

Nesta's heart sank, as her friend showed her a video that she had hoped to never see again. They both watched Darren's video in silence, whilst Catrin covered her mouth to hide an amused smile. The footage of the lakeside rant caused its star of the show to cringe, and, in that moment, she wanted the chair to swallow her whole.

"Ah, yes." Nesta swallowed a heavy gulp. "I can explain that one…" She let out a deep sigh. "Well, actually, no. I can't explain it. I haven't the foggiest when it comes to this online world. It is what it is."

Catrin was no longer hiding her smile. "It is what it is."

"Let me guess," said Nesta. "Is something like that against school policy as well?"

The deputy head had to think about it. "Uh, actually, I'm not too sure. I'd have to check."

"Don't bother." The older woman stared at the online video, and she prayed for it to finish. "I won't be doing anything like *that* again. I can promise you that."

"Shame," said Catrin, placing her phone back on the kitchen counter. "I thought you had rather good screen presence."

Nesta scowled at her, although she secretly enjoyed the compliment. Her onscreen debut was likely to be her last, but, she had to admit, it *was* a little fun whilst it lasted. "I'm sure many would say that I'd be better suited to radio with this face."

Catrin gave her arm a playful prod. "Don't talk daft."

They both smiled and finished off their teas.

"So, who do you think did it?"

Nesta's question caused the deputy head to choke on her last mouthful. "Excuse me?"

"Dafydd Thomas," said the older woman, leaning forward with a mischievous smirk. "Who do you think killed him? Surely, you must have your own theories."

"Nesta!" Catrin shook her head in disapproval. "I've never given it a moment's thought."

Her former mentor nodded. "Now I *know* you're lying. I'm sure everyone on the staff payroll has a theory."

"I barely knew the man." Catrin tried to resist her friend's ability to tempt her into opening up. She was generally quite a private person and rarely discussed her thoughts and feelings unless she had to. "If anything," she said, "I knew Dafydd more as a teenager — as you probably did."

"Exactly," said Nesta. "But your memory is a lot better than mine these days. Can you think of anyone from that era who is still working now? Who may have disliked the lad?"

Catrin searched the most dormant parts of her mind, and it made her uncomfortable, yet, at the same time, it gave her a strange, forbidden pleasure. "I suppose there was one person who stood out. But there are a lot of the old crew still there."

Nesta knew she had her now. "Go on..."

It almost hurt the deputy head to utter the name: "Arwel Maddocks."

"Arwel Maddocks?" Out of all the names that Nesta had expected to hear, Arwel Maddocks was not one of them. "But he was a pupil."

"You never said he had to be a teacher," said Catrin. "Besides, Arwel is a teacher now. He works at the school."

"He *does*?"

The younger woman nodded. "He's the chemistry teacher. Has been for a while."

"I had no idea. How did I not know that?"

Catrin stared at her dumbfounded friend and smiled. "You don't always know everything, Nesta."

"I suppose not." The retired English teacher pictured a spectacled young man sitting in the corner of her class. Arwel had been a very quiet, studious pupil that would never say boo to a goose. "What makes you suspect him?"

The deputy head became very nervous all of a sudden. "Now, I never once said that I *suspected* him of anything."

Nesta sighed. "Alright, calm down. This is completely off the record. I won't tell a soul."

"You asked me if there was anyone I knew who *disliked* Dafydd," said Catrin. "Well, I used to teach both of them in my class, and I know for a fact that Arwel did *not* like Dafydd Thomas one bit." She began picturing the quiet young man herself and experienced that same pity she had felt all of those years ago. "Arwel was a bit of an easy target, I suppose. He didn't seem to have any close friends. He wasn't athletic, and there was always an ailment of some kind that caused him to miss school. He was quite a sickly teenager."

"I hadn't really noticed," said Nesta, who was surprised at her own lack of awareness; she was normally quite observant. "I feel terrible."

"Nobody really noticed Arwel," said Catrin. "That was the problem. I think that, maybe, I saw a little bit of myself in him. I wasn't exactly popular when I was in school, and people gave me a hard time, too."

"Teenagers can be cruel."

Catrin nodded, trying to shake away the painful memories. "One person who I *did* notice giving him a hard time was Dafydd. It was just little things to start with, you know, the usual: chucking things at him from across the classroom when he thought I wasn't looking, making snide remarks when he tried to answer a question, passing notes around the class..."

"Notes?"

"Just childish stuff. Drawing rude pictures with Arwel's name underneath and getting other pupils to sneak it around until it reached him. Dafydd even tried to blame it on Arwel, once, when I caught him at it." Catrin shook her head. "That poor lad. Then, one day, I caught Dafydd and his friends gathered around Arwel in the corridor outside the science labs. I was their form teacher at one point, you see, so I always felt a certain degree of responsibility over the pair of them."

Nesta nodded. "I know the feeling. I used to treat my own form class like they were my own children. You often get them on their first day of school, see them morph from children into young adults. Then, a few years later, the whole cycle starts again."

"Yes," said Catrin. "It makes you realise how short life really is."

"You were saying about Arwel?"

"Oh, yes." Catrin placed her mind back to the moment outside the science labs. "They were all gathered around him, teasing and taunting, making jokes at his expense. I mean, they were in sixth form by this point. It was ridiculous. Arwel took it all on the chin and just stood there against the radiator. They didn't hear me coming, and I'd seen enough. That's when I decided to report it to Dyfrig Thomas."

Nesta remembered Dyfrig Thomas very well. He was a head teacher who ruled with an iron fist, a teacher with a style from a bygone era. He also happened to be Dafydd Thomas' father.

"That can't have been easy," she said.

"It wasn't," said Catrin. "But I didn't notice any more bullying after that day. Of course, that doesn't mean it wasn't going on behind closed doors."

"Quite," said her old friend. "So, Arwel is a teacher now?"

"Oh, yes. He's a fully-grown man now."

"Interesting..."

Nesta pondered over her new pieces of information and tried to decide whether it was socially acceptable to have a fourth cake. In the end, she had come to the conclusion that it certainly was and reached for another without the slightest hint of remorse.

CHAPTER 13

Nesta stared down at her completed one-thousand-piece jigsaw puzzle and sighed. It was always an anti-climactic moment, and, as with most things in life, the journey was far more satisfying than the end result. The landscape view of Blackpool Beach didn't quite have the same impact as it had done on her honeymoon, but it offered at least a few seconds of escapism. If she tried to imagine hard enough, Nesta could just about hear the distant cries of seagulls.

It was the second puzzle that week, and she was just about to attempt another one, when the doorbell rang.

Netsa made the short walk over to the front door with a certain degree of apprehension. She wasn't expecting any visitors, and, as the sun outside had already begun to set, there was unlikely to be any deliveries at this time.

"Hari!" she cried. "Will you be quiet!"

The excited Jack Russell circled her legs, until the door swung open to reveal a disgruntled-looking teenager in a black hoodie.

"Oh," said Nesta. "It's you."

Darren Price frowned at her underneath his wild fringe. "You tricked me."

The woman at her front door was stumped, until he lifted up an old Agatha Christie paperback. "Ah, yes."

"Where's the rest of it?" Darren asked, flicking through the pages. "I got to the end, and the last few pages are gone."

"Are you really still reading that thing?" Nesta asked. "I thought *I* was a slow reader.."

Darren was losing his patience. "Who was it? Who killed Ratchett?"

Nesta smiled. "I'm impressed. I never expected you to actually read it. So I removed the ending to see if you'd notice. And you did! Congratulations. You passed the test."

"Test?!" Darren snapped. "I don't need no test. Why didn't you think I would read it? I'm not daft."

Nesta shrugged. "Most of my former pupils never actually *read* their reading assignments. That's why I always had to go through it all again in class. You just get used to it after a while. But I suppose, every now and again, a pig does fly."

"Well, now I'm left hanging." Darren chucked the book into a nearby plant pot. "Are you gonna tell me, or what?"

The teacher smiled. "I think you better come inside and read it for yourself."

Darren stepped into the woman's front porch with the trepidation of a weary cat. "This isn't another twisted prank, is it? Nobody else knows I'm here."

"That's good," said Nesta, leading him through into the living room. "Because kidnapping a teenager is *exactly* what I need after an entire lifetime of trying to teach the rotten things."

"Hey?!" Darren froze in the doorway with a look of horror.

Nesta groaned. "I'm joking, you stupid boy — now, come on! Do you want to know the killer or not?" She reached into her dresser drawer and pulled out some crumpled pages. "Here," she said, handing them over.

The young man took the pieces of paper as though they were a sacred treasure map whilst, at the same time, not quite knowing what to do with them.

"Go on," said Nesta, pointing to an armchair. "Have a seat."

Darren begrudgingly sat himself down and began frantically reading. His eyes darted from side to side, scanning the small text until he reached the last page.

His host waited patiently for the final reaction which came with a sudden gasp.

"No way!"

The retired teacher grinned. "Ah, to be young again. I can't remember the first time I read *Murder On The Orient Express*. In fact, I'm pretty sure the ending was already ruined for me."

Her guest sat back in his chair and tried to process what he had just read. "I didn't see *that* one coming. I was pretty sure I had the killer down."

"You've not seen anything yet," said Nesta, pointing to her book collection. "Wait until you read *The Murder Of Roger Ackroyd*."

"Ackroyd?" asked Darren. "Like the pyjama factory in Bala?"

"Uh, no. They're not related."

The teenager stood up and headed over to the bookcase. He had never seen so many titles with the word 'murder' in all of his life. It was almost slightly disturbing to him that a person was *this* obsessed with murder mysteries, and now he was standing in their living room.

Nesta watched him peruse her private library with a certain sense of pride. "Ah, good choice."

Darren studied the colourful book cover in his hand. "Another Agatha lady book?"

"No, that's Agatha Raisin. She's a fictional character by M. C. Beaton."

The young man scratched his head. "Talk about confusing." He reached for *The Murder Of Roger Ackroyd*. "I'll take this one for now."

"Oh, will you?" Nesta raised her eyebrow. "So, I run a library now?"

Darren blushed. "Only if you don't mind, like. And only if there's no pages missing this time." He held the paperback under his arm and saw the jigsaw puzzle on the table. "You must have a lot of time on your hands."

"Says the person who spends his free time loitering around high street monuments?" Nesta folded up her arms and tried not to be too insulted. She watched the man casually head back over to her sofa and sit back down to read the blurb of his new book. He hadn't even noticed that there was a Jack Russell lying down beside him, and she was looking forward to his reaction when he realised.

"How are the true crime videos going?" she asked.

"I haven't really had time to do any more," he said without taking his eyes off the book.

Nesta nodded. "Well, you *are* very busy."

"I'm thinking of starting a podcast instead," said Darren.

"A *what*?"

"It's for people to listen to other people talk and that. They're really popular. It's all the rage now."

"So, basically, Radio Four."

Darren gave it some thought. "Uh, yeah, I suppose it is a bit like the radio."

It was hard for the retired woman not to be cynical. "Gosh, hasn't technology come a long way!"

Nesta was about to ask if he was leaving soon, but couldn't muster up the energy and wandered back over to her puzzle.

They both sat in silence for a while, until Darren lowered the book in his hand.

"Who do you think killed Dafydd Thomas?" he asked.

The woman nearby was shocked by the abrupt question and turned to face him. "I beg your pardon?"

"Dafydd Thomas," said Darren with an excited look on his face. "I can't stop thinking about it. It's like one of these books." He lifted up the paperback and chuckled. "The Murder Of Dafydd Thomas... by Agatha Price."

"I think Agatha Griffiths has a better ring to it," said Nesta with a cough. "Only there aren't any Belgium detectives around here to solve this one."

"What about you?" asked Darren.

Nesta stared at him. "What *about* me?"

He pointed at the bookshelf. "Well, you've read enough of those to know how it all works. *And* you've got plenty of time on your hands."

The teacher was trying to work out whether to be flattered or insulted. "I appreciate the kind words, but I do have a life, you know." Darren did not seem convinced. "Why do I get the impression that you want this case solved just so you can find out who did it?"

The teenager considered her question and nodded. "Pretty much, yeah. It's driving me nuts. Like when you ripped out those pages. Why can't they just find out who did it and just tell us?"

"You *do* know that real-life crimes are very different from works of fiction?" Nesta asked. "Plenty of crimes never get solved, and when they do, it's never that interesting."

Hari's loud bark caused the young man to jump out of his seat. His host tried to hide her amusement. "Don't worry," she said. "Hari's just seen a cat through the window. It always gets him excited."

Darren glanced over at the furry face staring at him, and he could have sworn the dog was smiling.

"I hope it was one of the teachers," he said.

"Excuse me?" Nesta asked, slightly offended.

"Dafydd Thomas' murder — it would be cool if one of the teacher's got sent down. Especially the biology one. I hate biology."

"I can assure you that 'cool' would not be the word to describe a teacher getting sent to prison for murder." Nesta paused for a moment. "And I'd only be the one having to substitute them. There's not a chance I'm teaching anyone biology."

"I wouldn't worry," said Darren. "I can't see Mrs Richards committing any murders."

Nesta tried to picture the biology teacher, the timid and introverted Liz Richards, standing over a body with an axe. It was always the quiet ones, she thought.

"What about the chemistry teacher?" she asked.

Darren looked up at her in surprise, and Nesta suddenly realised that she might have said too much.

"Mr Maddocks?"

"Forget I said anything," said Nesta. She was in enough trouble already without starting any rumours.

"He does always seem really stressed," said Darren.

"Chemistry teachers often are. It must be working with all those explosive substances all the time. It can make a person very jumpy."

"To be honest," Darren added, "I don't think Mr Maddocks even likes teaching young people in the first place."

Nesta watched him place his grubby trainers up on her coffee table. "Really?" she asked. "I can't for the life of me imagine why."

CHAPTER 14

Arwel Maddocks counted the row of test tubes for a third time. *Surely*, that would be enough, he thought to himself. The science lab at *Bala Secondary School*, with its tall wooden work benches and permanent smell of corrosive substances, was deathly quiet. It was exactly how the chemistry teacher liked it, and he still had another ten minutes until the next lesson.

The man wiped his glasses with the edge of his white lab coat and headed over to inspect his lesson plan. When he next turned around, there was another person in the room with him.

"Mrs Griffiths?" he asked.

Nesta stood there with her warm and friendly smile. She could often pull it out when necessary but only when it suited her most. "Mr Maddocks," she said. "It does feel funny being able to call you that."

Arwel gave a nervous laugh. "You can just call me Arwel, Mrs Griffiths — I mean —" The man paused. "Wait, I don't think I even know your first name."

"Nesta."

"Ah, yes. Nesta. I remember now."

"But you can call me Mrs Griffiths."

"Oh," said the awkward man.

His former English teacher groaned. "I'm joking, Arwel!"

There was another nervous laugh, and Arwel kept his eye on the clock.

"I know you have a class soon," said Nesta. "I won't be long. Just wanted to say hello. It's been a long time."

"Uh, yes." Arwel remembered her classes well and was always amazed by her natural ability to maintain order and control even back then. He could certainly learn a thing or two from the veteran.

"Are they all behaving?" she asked, wandering around the classroom and inspecting the various unfamiliar objects on display.

"The students?" The chemistry teacher asked. "Why, yes. Well —" He straightened up his glasses and coughed. "Most of the time. If I'm honest, the class I've got next can be a bit of a handful."

"Year Nine, by any chance?" Nesta watched the man nod. "Sounds about right. That's when they always tend to get a little tricky. They're no longer new, but they also haven't matured yet, either. Once they start choosing their GCSE subjects, at least you know they want to be in your class — to a certain degree."

"You never seemed to have any trouble from what I can remember," said Arwel. He looked at her as if she was somewhat of a hero.

"You have to set the tone from Day One," said Nesta, inspecting one of the gas taps sticking out from the desk. At least she didn't have to deal with Bunsen burners, she thought. "Too many teachers start raising their voices far too easily from the beginning. Once they see your limits, there's no going back. They'll walk all over you if they can. I learnt that from one of my mentors. There was this teacher called Richard Bramley. He had the quietest voice, and the pupils never made a sound. But, in the rare occasion he *did* snap, his voice would echo around the room. It was quite a frightening sight. Nobody dared test him. I think school pupils have a sixth sense about these things. They can tell, almost immediately, who they can and can't mess around with. It's all about commanding a certain degree of respect. It's not easy."

The chemistry teacher listened intently to every word. "I think it might be a little too late for me on that front."

"Nonsense!" Nesta moved closer to him and wanted to grab him by the shoulders. "You just need the confidence, that's all. You'll get there." She looked over at the blackboard and saw that it was littered with formulas she hardly recognised. "But never underestimate these young people. They can be crafty." She chuckled. "I remember when I was in school, we used to play this game, where we would try to train our teachers. We'd all be in on it." She pointed towards the blackboard. "Every time the teacher moved to the left-hand side of the class, we would all pretend to tune out and stop listening. Then, when they moved to the right-hand side, we would act all attentive and keen." She clapped her hands in excitement. "It worked every time! We'd have those teachers marching back and forth all the way through the lesson. It was marvellous!" Nesta turned to Arwel and saw that he wasn't nearly as amused. "If not a little childish, of course. I would never condone that kind of immature behaviour nowadays."

"Unfortunately," said Arwel. "The pupils aren't nearly as sophisticated with *their* misbehaviour."

The more experienced teacher saw the pain in his eyes and could understand. "Times have certainly changed," she said. "You were very well-behaved if I remember rightly."

Arwel smiled. "I wasn't the sort of person who enjoyed attention. Positive or negative."

"Did you enjoy school?" Nesta asked.

"I wish I could say I did," said her former pupil. "But there were aspects I very much hated."

"And what were those?"

"The people," said Arwel. For some strange reason, he chuckled as if he were joking, but he knew that he wasn't, and the older teacher knew that too. "I've never been much of a social butterfly."

"Was there anyone who gave you a hard time?" Nesta was hoping for a name in particular.

"One person springs to mind." The chemistry teacher lost his warmth for a moment, and the reflection of the lights in his glasses hid away his eyes. "It doesn't feel appropriate to say his name. Especially after what happened."

"I may have an idea," said Nesta.

Arwel seemed surprised but then gave in to his complicated feelings. "We actually got on okay as adults," he said. "But in school he was a nightmare." The man saw his fellow teacher's stare. "You probably know who I'm talking about."

Nesta stepped forward and placed a hand on his shoulder. "It's alright. I can only imagine what it must have been like to work alongside the person who tormented you as a youngster."

"That's the thing," said Arwel. "He acted like it never happened. People don't often get to face their school bully as an adult, let alone call them a work colleague. When I found out that he was joining us, I couldn't sleep for days. After all these years, I thought I'd moved on. But those feelings were still there — the same feelings I used to have on a Sunday night — they were coming back to haunt me."

"He didn't show any remorse?" asked Nesta. She could see the man had let his guard down a lot quicker than she had expected and it made her regret the visit altogether.

"I don't think he even remembered any of it," said the chemistry teacher. "In fact, he barely remembered who I was. I had to remind him. Pretty soon, he was joking around like we were mates." The man removed his glasses to reveal a pair of tired eyes. "You would think that would make everything okay, but it didn't. I was so confused, emotionally. All these years I'd tried to imagine what I'd do if I ever saw him again, and never in a million years would I have predicted *that*. I thought about him on a regular basis, and he probably hadn't given me a second thought. It was just too hard to process."

"Did you ever think about telling him?"

Arwel shook his head. "I couldn't bring myself to do it. Next thing I know, he was found dead." He rubbed his eyes, which had turned a dark shade of pink. He prayed that they'd return to normal before his pupils arrived. They would spot that straight away. "Now he'll never know how he used to make me feel. Not telling him was the worst mistake I've ever made. I'll regret it forever."

They were interrupted by the screams of a loud school bell. Arwel snapped out of his reflective trance and straightened up his posture.

Nesta couldn't help but take pity on the man and grabbed him by the arms. "Chin up, Mr Maddocks." She waited for him to make eye contact. "You can't let it spoil the rest of your life. None of this was your fault." The woman pointed to the closed door, and they could hear the distant cries of approaching students. "You've got a class-load of pupils arriving here any second. Think about how you were at their age. You can't change the past, but you do have a chance to affect their future." She let out a deep breath. "I don't often admit this... but, it's all worth it in the end — even if it's just for a single pupil."

Arwel stared back at her, as she released that firm grip and stepped away. The chemistry teacher nodded. "Thank you, Mrs Griffiths. I appreciate it."

Nesta gave him a playful wink. "Just don't you dare repeat what I just said to anyone," she said. "I'd hate for people to think that I was ever that sentimental. Nobody must know that Nesta Griffiths has a heart, you hear me?"

"Your secret's safe with me," said Arwel. He watched her disappear through the back door and tried to prepare himself for what was to come. It was time to unlock the gates and let in his horde of wild animals, only this time he felt ready.

Nesta could still hear the echoes of rowdy teenagers, as she descended the staircase from the first floor science labs. Her work here was done.

CHAPTER 15

Nesta paced back and forth at the front of her old classroom as if she had never left. In this lesson, she had been tasked with the responsibility of covering Year Ten English, and it was like slipping on a pair of old shoes. At last, she thought, a subject she could teach with her eyes closed.

Sitting on her desk was a paperback copy of the play *An Inspector Calls* by J. B. Priestley. It was a text that she knew inside and out. "Hello, old friend," she muttered to herself.

"Have you all read this play?" Nesta asked. She looked out towards the room full of gloomy faces. "I'll take it from your silence that you haven't."

A pupil called Mared raised her hand. "We've only just started it, Miss."

"I'm glad one of you can speak," said the supply teacher. "How fortunate you all are." She picked up the book and held it out to them. "You're in for a big treat. This is a story about actions and consequences. As you'll all know, all of our actions have consequences — no matter who we are."

"Doesn't look like there's much action," said Eben, who lifted up the faded, old cover from his desk and caused the rest of the room to snigger.

Nesta frowned in disapproval. "If you're looking for a character that runs around with a machine gun, calling himself Bruce Willis, then, no. I'm afraid you'll be greatly disappointed." There was more laughter. "But I can assure you that there's plenty in here to invigorate and shock you. Even you, Eben." She pointed to the young man. "And seeing as you're so vocal today, perhaps you can read out the main part — the mysterious Inspector Goole."

Her suggestion caused Eben to cringe. "Nah, you're alright, Miss."

"Am I now?" asked the teacher. "I'm glad you think I'm alright. But that's not what I asked. I look forward to your star performance."

Sitting at the back of the class was a pupil who had been watching this supply teacher with great fascination. Darren Price had recently got to know Nesta Griffiths a little, but he had yet to see her conduct a lesson. Watching this experienced veteran holding court to his fellow pupils surprised him, and it was like witnessing a strange alter ego. A far cry from Batman or Superman, Nesta Griffiths — the teacher — was still a force to be reckoned with, and he was glad that she hadn't singled him out yet.

English had become one of his favourite lessons as of late, but not because of the Shakespeare or Dickens. This was the one and only class where he could sit next to someone he had been trying to get to know for quite some time. The main problem was, the two teenagers had yet to even speak with each other. Lowri Meredydd had a beauty that distracted many pupils from their lessons. When sitting beside a window in the afternoon sun, she almost resembled an angel (at least, she did to Darren).

The two pupils could not have been any more different; Darren had hair that was as wild as a blackberry bush and a hoodie that had been worn almost everyday since it had been bought. Lowri, on the other hand, had the hair of a thoroughbred pony and neatly-pressed clothes that seemed to fit the young woman perfectly. Together, Darren and Lowri were like either ends of a triple-A battery and both had less in common than a midwife and an undertaker. Still, their differences had not deterred Darren in the slightest, and he hoped that, one day, he could muster up the courage to utter his first few words to Lowri Meredydd. What these words were likely to be, however, was a mystery even to him.

"Are you still with us, Mr Price?"

Nesta's words caused Darren to jump, and he looked up to see that all eyes were now on him. "Uh, yeah. Why?"

"You seem a little distracted back there," said Nesta. "Are you paying attention? Good. You can read the part of Arthur Birling." Darren groaned into his hoodie. "Lowri," she continued, "you can be Sybil — Arthur Birling's wife."

This last little detail gave Darren a sudden burst of enthusiasm, and he prepared himself to live out a fantasy that he never knew he'd had.

∽

THE STAFF ROOM at lunchtime was surprisingly busy for a change, and when Nesta entered to seek out her tupperware from the fridge, she was a little overwhelmed. Her favourite chair had been taken, and, with the lack of any old and familiar faces, she now had to choose a spot which involved sitting next to a teacher she barely knew.

It was at this moment that she spotted a familiar face in the corner of the room, and she breathed a sigh of relief.

"Thank God," she said, sitting herself down next to Catrin, whose head was buried in a book. "I almost had to sit next to that crazy art teacher."

"Yes," said the deputy head. "It's annoying when you come in here for some peace and quiet."

Nesta gave the smirking woman a playful nudge with her shoulder. "Very funny." She began munching on her pre-cooked pasta and gazed around the room. There were plenty of other familiar faces and some that she had yet to speak to since her return: Liz Richards, the biology teacher; Siwan Rowlands, the French teacher; Megan Mason, the drama teacher. Almost everyone in the entire room seemed to be avoiding any hint of conversation, and the mood was very sombre. Nesta remembered a time when all of her peers used to sit around in a giant circle with their mugs of tea, shooting the breeze and venting their frustrations. But that culture seemed to be long gone, and it was a sad sight to see.

After talking away for the best part of five minutes without a response, Nesta turned to see that Catrin was very much still engrossed in her book. "So, as I was saying, it's a shame that the bakery on the high street doesn't exist anymore after the fire. Terrible shame." She waited for a reaction, until Catrin eventually caught her staring.

"Hmh?"

Nesta sighed. "See, I knew you weren't listening. You love that bakery."

The deputy head closed her book and blushed. "Sorry, Nesta. I've been obsessed with this new series. I just can't seem to put it down." She handed her the battered paperback. "Here, you can borrow it, if you like. It's the first book in the series. I've already read it three times."

The older woman cautiously inspected the mysterious cover, which consisted of little more than a flowery pattern and a giant title in the middle: In Wolf's Clothing by Ela Crowbourne.

"It's in the romance genre," said Catrin.

"I don't usually do romance," said Nesta.

"Neither do I. But this is a bit different. I know that murder mysteries are normally your guilty pleasure."

Nesta turned her head with a frown. "Who ever said I felt guilty?"

Catrin laughed, and they both continued with their portable lunches.

"Have you had your chat with Johnny?" the deputy head asked.

"Not yet," Nesta muttered with a shudder. "He'll see me this afternoon." She munched on her tasteless pasta. "I did speak to our Mr Maddocks, though."

"Nesta!"

"What?"

They both looked around the room and lowered their voices.

"It was just an informal chat," said Nesta. "Nothing more."

"So is he on your list as well now?" asked Catrin.

The supply teacher huffed. "I don't have a list."

Catrin shook her head. "Yeah, right. Whatever you say." She nibbled on her rice cake. "So who's at the top?" It was now Nesta's turn to look surprised, and the deputy head gave her an innocent shrug. "What? I'm allowed to be curious."

"Shame on you," said Nesta, tutting away, with an amused smile. "Well, I don't think Arwel's up there."

"Doesn't seem like the type?" asked Catrin.

"Doesn't have much of a motive. He said that Dafydd was perfectly friendly with him as a colleague. People change, I suppose. Others don't." Nesta watched as maths teacher Berwyn Lewis could be seen laying out a row of crackers in a perfect line over in the distance. The obsessive-compulsive individual proceeded to then prepare his slices of cheese with a knife he'd brought from home. She tried to picture the same knife being used as a murder weapon, until she shook the unpleasant thought out of her head.

"Doesn't mean that Arwel had let everything go," Catrin said.

Nesta gave her another judgemental glare. "I thought you weren't accusing anybody?"

"I'm not!" Catrin saw a couple of teachers looking and went a bright shade of red before lowering her voice back down. "You just can't rule any of these things out, that's all. I might not read murder mysteries, but I know the unpredictability of human behaviour."

"And here comes the cranberry sauce," said Nesta.

Catrin saw that her friend was more preoccupied with the maths teacher's next move, and, just as predicted, Berwyn Lewis began placing carefully measured dollops of cranberry sauce on his row of cheese and crackers.

Nesta smiled. "Right on cue."

CHAPTER 16

John Glyn (or Johnny, as he liked to be called), the head teacher of *Bala Secondary School*, sat on the edge of his desk as if he was casually chatting to an old friend. His informal leadership style, something that he had adopted from the beginning of his short tenure in charge, was an approach that he took great pride in. He was, in his own mind, at least, a man of the people and determined to do away with some of the old fashioned traditions of his predecessors.

The young man's amused smirk was a permanent fixture on his long, chiselled face, and, at that very moment in time, it was quite appropriate — for he was genuinely amused by the situation he now found himself in.

Summoned to the headmaster's office like a naughty schoolgirl, Nesta sat in the chair before him, holding back her tongue with gritted teeth. It hadn't been that long ago that a teenage Johnny Glyn had found himself sitting in the naughty chair of her *own* classroom — and the smug headteacher knew it. Nesta would have given anything in that moment to reach across and grab him by the earlobe, demanding that he sit in a proper chair and not on his desk.

"This feels strange, doesn't it?"

Nesta re-adjusted herself in the uncomfortable chair. "Is this going to take long?"

"Mrs Griffiths," said Johnny. "Or Nesta. Can I call you Nesta now?"

"You can call me Mrs Griffiths."

The man blushed. "Right, okay. Well, I think you know why you're here."

"Because I made the barmy decision to come back to teaching?"

The headteacher let out a forced laugh. "No, no, no. We're very glad to have you back." He began playing with his stylish wristwatch. "The reason I called this meeting is because —"

"You want to give me an earful?" asked Nesta.

"Absolutely not. I wouldn't dare. You've had a lot more experience doing that than I have." He exposed his bright white teeth with a wide smile and wondered whether she remembered their little talks after class. She *did* remember. "Listen, Mrs Griffiths, I'm not here to tell an old grandma how to suck eggs —"

"I beg your pardon?"

For a split second, Johnny's smile vanished and was replaced with a terror in his eyes. "That is the expression, isn't it? Eggs, grandmother, sucking..."

"You could have chosen a saying without the word grandmother," Nesta snapped. "I may have been retired for a while, but I'm not on a zimmer frame just yet."

The apologetic headteacher lifted up his hands. "Forgive me," he said. "I'd hate for you to think that I'm being ageist." The man jumped to his feet and began pacing up and down in front of his desk. "Let me cut to the chase. I just wanted to have this little chat because I've had a few reports that you might be a little... distracted."

"Distracted?"

"By the passing of one of our colleagues."

"You mean — murder?"

Nesta's blunt choice of words shocked the headteacher. "Uh, well, we don't know that for sure. But, still, whatever the cause of death might have been, I hear you've been going around asking a lot of questions."

"Is that a crime?" Nesta asked. She could see the young man was getting flustered, and she was enjoying every moment.

"It's making people uncomfortable," said Johnny. "I know you're probably very upset — we all are. Including myself."

"Remind me of your relationship with Dafydd again?"

Johnny realised that he was slowly losing control of his meeting. He had hoped to be the one asking all of the questions, but now he felt like he was the one defending himself. "Dafydd and I go way back, obviously. We played football together."

"Ah, yes." Nesta nodded. "That's right. Is that why you hired him as the sports teacher?"

"We had a very rigorous hiring process for that role," said Johnny, whose pacing was becoming quicker with every question. "There was no favouritism going on. He was basically the best man for the job."

"Sure," said the supply teacher. "The best — *man*. Obviously."

Johnny gave up trying to defend his decision and sat himself down in his chair. He suddenly felt a lot safer now that there was a wide desk between him and his former English teacher.

"Look," he said. "It's all a very sensitive time around this school with what's happened, and I'm just asking everyone to just keep their heads down and carry on as best as they can."

"You want me to stop asking questions," said Nesta. "I understand. It's a fair request."

The tired headteacher breathed a sigh of relief.

"But let me ask you this — wasn't Dafydd best friends with Geraint Owen back in school?"

Johnny's heart sank. He knew this meeting was going to be a waste of time. "Well, yes, sort of. Actually, it's a little complicated." The man squirmed in his chair, and it pained him to even discuss what he was about to say next. "Dafydd and I were childhood friends. Our fathers were very close."

"Your father was friends with Dyfrig Thomas?" Nesta asked. She knew Dyfrig Thomas herself, after all, and it hadn't seemed that long ago since the former headteacher was sitting at that very same desk.

"They were childhood friends themselves," said Johnny. "One became a headmaster, and the other a local MP."

"Yes, that's right." Nesta had almost forgotten about Nedw Glyn. She had once voted for him in a local election and always thought he was a charming individual. "I'm sure your father is very proud to see where you are now."

Johnny shrugged. "I think Dyfrig Thomas would be very proud. According to Dafydd, his dad had always been keen for him to follow in his footsteps. I suppose you can only have one headteacher."

Nesta had a sudden thought. "Wait a minute... is this why I'm here for my verbal warning? Did Geraint put you up to this? A favour between old pals? A big boy's club!"

The head teacher shook his head and scoffed. "Mrs Griffiths, please. I never said this was a verbal warning. And besides, Geraint Owen and I are definitely not friends."

"But you and Dafydd were?" Nesta asked.

"Yes, as children. We were obsessed with football. That's all we used to do with each other growing up. Then, in secondary school, things changed. Dafydd started hanging around with Geraint and his crew. I never had anything in common with that lot. Neither did Dafydd, really. They were all raised on farms.

But they were popular, I suppose." The man pulled a face that implied he had never quite recovered from his separation. "He used to pretend that I didn't even exist sometimes. I'd try and find him in the playground, and I swear he was hiding. I even tried to join that clique of his, but there didn't seem to be any room for a townie like me."

"Dafydd grew up in the town, didn't he?"

Johnny nodded. "He kept leaning on the fact that his mother's family were all farmers. Not that he knew the first thing about that world! He was also the headteacher's son, so I guess they thought he was useful to have on board. I was a good footballer, but that didn't seem to count for anything with that group. They all liked rugby. In the end, I took the hint and found my own group. Best thing I ever did. At least they all played football."

"That must have hurt a little," said Nesta, studying the man's face.

"It definitely stung at first," said Johnny. "I was pretty upset after a while. But it all just showed Dafydd's true colours in the end. He had no loyalty to anyone. I think it left him quite lonely in the long term. He lost all his friends in the end."

"How is your father these days?" Nesta asked. "I haven't seen him campaigning for years."

Johnny smiled. "Politics wasn't really for him. He gave all that up a long time ago. He's working for *Gwynedd Council* nowadays."

"And he's still in touch with Dyfrig?" The teacher could still picture her old boss, sitting in the chair in front of her with his large moustache. "I haven't seen that man in years."

"Dyfrig is still around," said Johnny. "He's quite into his gardening. He lives over on Eryl Street."

Nesta made a mental note and stood up from her chair. "I assume we're finished here? If you don't mind, I have some very important business to attend to." She felt Catrin's paperback in the bottom of her handbag and looked forward to getting better acquainted with her new reading material.

"Uh, yes." The nervous headteacher stood up as though he were being dismissed by the queen. "I appreciate your time, Mrs Griffiths. I think it's been a very productive meeting."

"*Very* productive," said Nesta.

Johnny scurried over and gave her the most awkward handshake she had ever received. "Keep up the good work, won't you, Mrs Griffiths?"

Nesta headed over to the door, and, before she left the room, turned back around to utter her final words to him: "Call me Nesta."

CHAPTER 17

"There you are!" Nesta cried, as she came marching toward the school reception desk with determined strides. She had closed the book on her latest paperback only the night before and had a real bone to pick with the person who lent it to her.

Catrin Jones saw the older woman approaching and had a fair idea of what the issue might be. "Is everything alright?"

"Don't use that innocent tone with me," said Nesta lifting up the book titled: *In Wolf's Clothing*. She realised that the receptionist on the other side of the counter had also caught a glimpse of her reading material, and Nesta quickly hid the book behind her back. "Can I have a word in private?" she whispered.

Catrin rolled her eyes, and they both walked over to the corner on the other side of the reception.

"You didn't tell me —" Nesta looked over their shoulders to make sure that nobody was in earshot. "You didn't tell me that this book was... erotic."

The younger woman couldn't help but giggle and held a hand over her own mouth. "Did you seriously just use the word *erotic*?"

"Is that not what you would call it?" asked Nesta.

"No!"

"You told me it was a romance novel."

Catrin shook her head in embarrassment. "They call it *spicy* romance. It's still romance. Just a bit... spicier."

"Spicy?" Nesta paused as a fellow teacher walked past before continuing. "This isn't a curry recipe we're talking about."

"I'd say it's pretty mild," said Catrin. "Technically, it's a paranormal spicy romance."

"There's nothing paranormal about what those two main characters were doing by the end," Nesta snapped.

"So you finished it?"

The older woman paused. "Well, uh, yes. I always finish a book. Plus I wanted to find out what happened to Raven."

Catrin nodded. "Oh, sure, yeah. Just you wait until you see what happens to him in the *next* book."

"He's in the next book?"

The deputy head refused to answer her question and left her hanging in the corner of the reception. "Have a good morning, Mrs Griffiths!" she called out.

Gwen Williams was sitting behind her counter, peering over her glasses, with an intrigued face. The receptionist had seen all sorts from her little booth and was, in her own mind, the eyes and ears of the school.

"Did you find that form I was looking for?" Nesta asked her, leaning against the counter with her book still in hand.

"Ah, yes. I did, actually." Gwen smiled and went over to fetch a sheet of paper from one of her many trays.

"Thank you," said the teacher, studying the document with a repulsed expression. It had seemed that the amount of paperwork now required in her role had practically doubled since she had retired, and she was about ready to see if her old paper shredder still worked.

"You're in for a treat," said Gwen.

Nesta stared at her. "Excuse me?"

The receptionist grinned. "I'm on Book Seven. It gets even better."

The teacher glanced from side to side and leant forward against the desk. "Are you really talking about *In Wolf's Clothing*?"

Gwen winked at her. "It's always nice to find a fellow fan. Welcome to the club."

"Oh," said Nesta. "I won't be reading anymore. I can assure you of that."

"That's a shame," Gwen muttered with a change of tone in her voice. She almost seemed offended. "You'll never get to find out who the elders are. Then there's the whole Elijah redemption storyline."

Nesta tried to resist her burning curiosity and shook away the temptation to ask more. "I'm more partial to the crime genre. I find detectives and murderers more interesting." Her desire to shock the receptionist into silence had worked but only for a moment.

"There's enough of that going on in real life," said Gwen with a shudder. "I mean, look what happened to Dafydd Thomas. And they still haven't solved that one."

"It's not an easy case to solve," said the teacher.

The receptionist scoffed. "I'd say whoever *did* murder him was pretty stupid. If you're going to fake a suicide, don't knock him over the head first. Did that person really think they'd get away with it *that* easily?"

"They have so far," Nesta muttered.

"That goes to show the competence of our police service," said Gwen.

Nesta thought about Constable Aled Parry and decided not to argue with her. "Who do you think killed him?"

Gwen thought she'd never ask. It was a very lonely post as the sole receptionist of a secondary school, and she never usually got the chance to share her thoughts. "I've got a few theories," she said.

"I'm sure you have…"

The receptionist placed her forearms against the counter and leant forward with an excited grin. "But what I'm more interested in is the affair."

Nesta's initial scepticism was immediately washed away by a single word. "*Affair*? What affair?"

"You haven't heard about the affair rumours?" Gwen rocked back and forth in her chair. "They've been around way before Dafydd was found dead. Everyone knows about the affair."

The older woman was amazed how quickly a piece of information had gone from merely a "rumour" to something that "everyone" knew as fact. "You'll have to forgive me," she said. "Gossip isn't really my thing."

"I was the first to rumble them," the receptionist said, proudly.

And, presumably, the first to spread the rumours, Nesta thought to herself. "Were you really?"

"Oh, yeah." Gwen began playing with her fingernails. "Nothing gets past me in this school. I know everyone's secrets. I'm the first person people ring for a sick day, remember? I've heard it all. I'm the keeper of every white lie ever told. And everyone knows it."

As someone who had barely taken a sick day in her entire career, Nesta knew that she was in the clear as far as *those* were concerned. "So, who exactly was Dafydd having an affair with?"

The receptionist jiggled with excitement and leant over to whisper: "Megan Mason."

"The drama teacher?" Nesta asked.

Gwen immediately hushed her, not that there was anyone else around. "Careful, there are eyes and ears everywhere."

The teacher wanted to remind her that one of the perpetrators of this love affair was now dead and that he was unlikely to be worried about getting caught by this stage, but she humoured the younger woman with an apologetic wince and lowered her voice. "Is Megan married?"

Gwen shook her head. "Not anymore. I think she has three different sons from three different partners, so there was nothing to lose from her side."

"She seems quite young," said Nesta.

"So are her sons. I think they're all under ten."

"Oh. Well, I suppose not all of us can make the right choice the first time around."

The receptionist pulled a judgemental snarl. "Or the second or third…"

Nesta shook her head. "I don't know how people find the time for a second relationship on the side. I struggled with just the one. There's not enough hours in the day."

"I don't think this relationship was intended to be serious," said Gwen.

"Why do you say that?"

"They didn't hide it particularly well." The receptionist shrugged. "I think it was all based on lust. A Zachary and Arabella situation."

The teacher was startled by the reference to her recent steamy, paranormal romance novel. "You're comparing them to vampires?" she asked.

"Technically," said Gwen. "They're not vampires. They're demonic vessels."

Nesta rolled her eyes. The last time she checked, anyone who sucked other people's blood and flew around in the night were most definitely vampires. "I wasn't a fan of that subplot. There's no way Zachary would be stupid enough to get seduced by Arabella."

Gwen looked up at her and smiled. "What makes you think that I wasn't talking about Dafydd and Megan?"

CHAPTER 18

Nesta made the long journey down to the drama department with a slight sense of unease. She had been warned not to go around asking people uncomfortable questions, but the supply teacher didn't see the harm in introducing herself to someone she had yet to formally meet.

Megan Mason had started long after Nesta had retired and, by all accounts, was a rather eccentric person. Nesta had decided that *she* would be the judge of that, as she would hardly deem any of her colleagues "normal" by anyone's standards, including herself.

The sound of a familiar song echoed down the hallway, as she headed past the music department, where a violin lesson was in full swing. As much as she enjoyed the musical accompaniment to her walk, it also seemed that the pupil required a great deal more practice. After all, there was no worse instrument to play out of tune than one where the performer had to grind a stick across a series of strings. Her son had learnt to play the trumpet in his youth, and *that* had been bad enough.

As the music began to fade away, Nesta finally reached the open doorway of the drama department, where she was surprised to hear another type of music. The instruments themselves were hard to pinpoint, but it became clear that the sounds were intended to soothe and relax. Nesta had once heard such music at a garden centre near Ruthin and had almost nodded off whilst trying out a new bench.

She entered the room to find a woman in loose, colourful clothing, kneeling on a rolled-out floor mat whilst closing her eyes and breathing deeply. Nesta knocked against the wooden door frame and hoped that her interruption wouldn't startle the woman into a frantic seizure.

"Oh," said Megan, opening her eyes. "I didn't see you there."

Her visitor took a quick look around the room which consisted of very little but a large open space and a handful of chairs. It was unlike any other classroom she had visited and wondered how the teacher ever got any teaching done at all.

"Sorry to disturb you," she said. "I'm Nesta Griffiths."

Megan leapt onto her feet with an effortless motion that made the older woman very jealous. "*You're* Nesta?" she cried, running over in bare feet to shake her hand. "I've heard so much about you."

"That's concerning," said the supply teacher. "Nothing bad, I hope."

The drama teacher howled with laughter and seemed to have bundles of energy that the other woman would have paid good money for. Whatever Megan was on, Nesta would have taken a double-dose.

"Don't be silly!" Megan cried. "Come, come in! Make yourself at home. Have a sit down."

Nesta took another look at the minimal furniture and wondered where, exactly, the younger woman had expected her to sit. "It's okay, I'm happy standing." She pointed to the yoga mat. "Is this how you spend your lunch breaks? On the floor?"

Megan giggled. It seemed that she found everything

amusing and reminded Nesta of another teacher she had once worked with who would laugh at any given opportunity. If laughter was the best medicine, then both her and Megan were eternally cured.

"I wouldn't have it any other way," said the drama teacher. "It's important to prioritise our mindfulness and wellbeing these days, whenever we can."

"I couldn't agree more," said Nesta, who had spent her last lunch break munching on a pork pie whilst reading *The Daily Mirror*. "I've always wanted to try yoga or meditation but never quite got around to it. I suppose doing nothing takes a lot of time and energy. My late husband was probably a lot better suited to such things. He would have been quite happy to sit there and stare at the wall for hours if he had the chance. I used to constantly tell him that he had no sense of urgency." She let out a private chuckle. "He used to always joke about having it written on his tombstone. Morgan Griffiths: No Sense Of Urgency."

Nesta looked back at Megan and saw that her amusing memory had flown straight over her head. Instead of laughing with her, she placed a concerned hand on her shoulder.

"I'm so sorry about your loss," said the drama teacher.

"Oh, there's no need," said Nesta. "It was a few years ago." She felt a hand being placed against her chest.

"All wounds heal in time," said Megan. "We just have to do the best we can to speed up the process. Our hearts are a fragile thing."

Nesta cringed and tried to think of an appropriate response. "My stomach's a bit fragile, too. Not to mention my right knee!" Once again, she laughed alone.

"Hey!" Megan clapped her hands. "Did you want to join me?"

Her visitor returned the proposition with a perplexed stare.

As far as Nesta was aware, she was already in the room. "Join you for lunch?"

The drama teacher giggled. "For a session on the mat, silly!" She pointed to the floor, somewhere the older woman was not keen on getting more acquainted with. "I'm a qualified instructor in Hatha, Ashtanga and Transcendental, but I promise I won't charge you."

Nesta's body temperature rapidly began to rise, and she felt the sudden urge to run back up the corridor. "Oh, I really don't think —"

"Come on," said the drama teacher, grabbing her hand and pulling her to the centre of the room. "It won't take long. I promise you won't regret it. You said it yourself that you always wanted to give it a try."

The supply teacher found that she said a lot of things that she often regretted and that statement had been one of them. "My joints just aren't up to being stretched at the moment, and I pulled my back yesterday —"

Megan did not seem to take no for an answer and laughed. "I don't mean a full-on yoga session! I'm talking about some T.M."

Nesta tried to work out the initials and, with it being the start of the week, hoped that they stood for Takeaway-Mondays.

"T.M.?"

"Transcendental meditation!"

In Nesta's mind, the words sounded awfully close to a type of gender-altering procedure, something that she would have preferred over what was about to come.

"Technically, you need a personal mantra," Megan continued, "but we'll just stick with the breathwork for now."

"I'm already very good at breathing," Nesta assured her. "In fact, I can do it in my sleep."

"Nobody ever said that you were so funny, Nesta!" The

drama teacher howled again and encouraged her to kneel down on the mat.

Unfortunately for Nesta, the simple act of kneeling down was enough of an obstacle with her tight quads, and she could hear the crunching sound of her knees as they lowered down in position. As a regular church-goer, the only kneeling Nesta had done in recent times was to say her prayers, but at least her local church had adequate padding. She had always been grateful to be a christian rather than a buddhist, as the thought of crossing her legs in the lotus position made her hips hurt.

Now that she was kneeling on Megan's yoga mat, the uncomfortable supply teacher knew that she wasn't going anywhere in a hurry and decided that she might as well settle in for the long haul.

"Now," said Megan, "it's all about focusing on your breathing…"

Nesta took a deep breath and could hear the rattle of her congested sinuses. Every now and again, she peeked open her eyelids to make sure that she was still on planet earth and had not fallen foul of some cruel prank.

Megan was kneeling beside her and had the straightened posture of a meerkat. Unlike her fellow meditator, she kept her eyelids firmly closed. "In through the nose and out through the mouth… slow, deep breaths…"

The older woman surrendered to the moment and made a deliberate effort to give this method a chance. Several breaths later, and she felt as high as a kite but not in the way that felt pleasant. The deep inhalations had gone straight to her head, and she began to feel a little dizzy.

"Clear your mind," said Megan. "Focus on the single-act of your breathing and let go of any unwanted emotions."

There were plenty of unwanted emotions, Nesta thought, one of which involved the fear of her knees never working again, and, after a few minutes of excruciating boredom, her mind began to race with a swirl of distorted images. Soon, these vague shapes morphed into various faces of people who had come and gone from her life, culminating in the profile of her late husband. Morgan Griffiths smiled back at her, as though he were kneeling in the same room. A cosy warmth filled her entire body, and she had the same sensation of sliding into a hot bath.

Megan's commentary was now fading into the background, a distant echo behind a trail of personal thoughts. Lost in her comforting trance, Nesta was not prepared for what she was about to experience next. After the familiar face of her late husband, she was faced with the horrific image of Dafydd Thomas in a bed of shallow water. The man's eyes opened, suddenly, and caused Nesta to break her dreamlike state with an enormous gasp.

"Nesta!" Megan cried. "Are you alright?"

The woman beside her looked around as though she had been woken up from a deep sleep.

"Uh, yes." Nesta took a moment to shake herself back into the room. "I think I might have overdone it."

Megan placed her hands together and bowed her head. "Namaste, Nesta." She giggled. "That actually sounds a little funny! Namaste, Nesta!"

"Yes," said Nesta. "It's hysterical. Can you help me up, please?" She raised up her arms, as the slender woman pulled her back up to her feet.

"You did good for your first time," said Megan.

Nesta was not so sure. "I'm glad you didn't charge me for that. I'd be asking for my money back."

The drama teacher cackled. "There you go with that funny sense of humour of yours! Oh, I'm so glad I got to meet you!"

"Likewise," said the other teacher. "There was one little thing I wanted to talk to you about before I go."

"Absolutely!" Megan scurried over to her desk and grabbed an enormous smoothie bottle. "We can talk about anything. We've got a lot in common, you and me."

"We do?" Nesta followed her to the desk, which, unlike the rest of the room, was very cluttered.

Megan lifted up a printed copy of *Romeo and Juliet*. "We both teach Shakespeare! Not to mention plays in general. We're practically the same teacher!"

Nesta humoured her with a nod but would never have gone as far as to suggest that she and Megan were a carbon copy of each other. "Yes, I suppose there are similarities with the subjects we teach. Plays have always been on my syllabus, but I wouldn't say I was quite as practical with the text as you might be in here."

"I do love Shakespeare," said the drama teacher with a flick of her leg. "He's such a romantic."

"Apart from all the tragedies," said Nesta. "And the bloodshed."

"Yes, but who needs to focus on that? I've always been a hopeless romantic myself." Megan admired the cover of her favourite play. "I mean, what doesn't convey love more than a person poisoning themselves to be with them?"

"Relationships are certainly about sacrifice," Nesta muttered.

"Love, death... it's all part of the same, wonderful journey."

"Talking of death..." Nesta cleared her throat. "I hear that you were a friend of Dafydd Thomas?"

The drama teacher's beaming smile disappeared for a moment. "Oh, yes. I knew Dafydd."

"*How* well?" Nesta asked.

"Pretty well." Megan saw the woman's cynical stare and sighed. "Between you and me, you know, girl to girl —"

"English teacher to drama teacher?"

"Yes, exactly." The younger woman conveyed her first hint of sadness. It seemed that even Megan Mason was not immune to such an emotion. "Dafydd and I were involved with each other for a short while."

"*Involved?*"

"I'm sure you've heard the rumours," said Megan. "Even the pupils knew what was going on. I'd have the odd person shout out Dafydd's name in class to try and get a reaction. Dafydd was down here more times than he was in the staff room. It was inevitable people were going to notice."

"So you *did* have an intimate relationship," said Nesta.

Megan blushed. "It was just a bit of fun to start with. It was obvious we had chemistry, and he was always very flirty. I was single, so I didn't think we were doing anything wrong."

"But *he* wasn't single."

"No," said Megan. She hung her head in shame. "I still feel terrible about that. I didn't think to ask him about his own personal life, at least not to start with. He came on so strong that I couldn't imagine that he had a girlfriend. By the time I knew, we'd already formed this connection. And he was adamant that he was going to break up with his girlfriend." She stared at the *Romeo and Juliet* cover and chucked the text away across the desk. "I genuinely thought we were in love. And I *was* at the time. Then, one day, he gave me the cold shoulder. He said he wanted to call the whole thing off — whatever this thing was supposed to be. Pretty soon, I realised that it was just a physical attraction. He didn't *love* me."

Nesta saw the anger in her body, as her strong posture tightened. "He broke up with you?"

"I'm used to men letting me down," snapped Megan. "Although, it *did* hurt when I found out that he was getting engaged." She became suddenly aware of her sour mood and tried to regain her composure with a series of steady breaths. In a matter of seconds, her positive smile was back. "But, like I said before — all wounds heal in time."

"Our hearts are a fragile thing," said Nesta.

The drama teacher appreciated having another one of her favourite mantras quoted back to her. Before bidding her farewells, the English teacher picked up another text lying on the desk and admired the cover.

"If you're looking for another Shakespearean love story," she said, "perhaps you'd be better off with this one instead. It's not *Romeo and Juliet*, but at least it has a happy ending."

Nesta handed her the play, and Megan read the title with an understanding nod: *Much Ado About Nothing*.

CHAPTER 19

Police Constable Aled Parry was still recovering from a rather intense domestic call-out on Cae Bach Estate by the time his afternoon had rolled around. For some unknown reason, these types of incidents always seemed to happen at tail-ends of the day, and an early-morning physical altercation was not what the police officer had needed that day. There was no worse fight than a married couple on the rocks, and Mr and Mrs Farren had (almost literally) thrown the kitchen sink at each other.

It was therefore why Aled Parry was hoping that the second-half of his day would be as drama-free as possible. Unfortunately for him, however, that was when he saw the double-parked *Land Rover*.

Farmer Siôn Puw happened to be still eating his lunch, as he sat in the front seat of his *Land Rover* whilst sharing two Cornish pasties with his Sheepdog, Mott. As he prepared to take another bite of piping-hot goodness, a tapping sound made him grumble, and he reluctantly wound down his window to reveal the face of a local police officer.

"Is this your vehicle, sir?"

Aled jumped back in fright, as he was greeted by a barking Sheepdog.

"Mott!" Siôn cried. "Get down!" The dog's amused owner pushed his animal back towards the passenger seat. "Sorry about that, officer. He just loves the smell of bacon, that's all." The policeman frowned, and the farmer laughed before giving him a playful shove. "Lighten up, Ali! I'm only having a laugh!" He slapped the steering wheel and gave him a wicked grin. "How's the wife, by the way?" The man leant over. "Not that it's any of my business, mind, but, rumour has it, you two are... you know... having a bit of trouble."

Aled lifted up his hat and wiped down his forehead. "Where, uh... where did you hear that from?"

"Oh, you know what people are like. Your wife tells her friend — that friend tells *her* friend — the other friend tells my wife." Siôn shrugged. "It's a small town."

The police officer looked around to check if anyone was watching.

"Hey!" Siôn cried. "Have you tried wearing that smart uniform of yours in the bedroom? That should work wonders!" He howled with laughter, and the other man looked down at his police jumper.

"We're doing just fine," said Aled. "But thank you, Siôn. I appreciate the concern." He coughed into his hand. "Now, the reason I'm here is because your vehicle appears to be double-parked."

Siôn popped his head out of the window and looked down at the two yellow lines. "Why, so it is! Ha! Well spotted. That must be your special police training kicking in there, Ali."

"I'm afraid I'm going to have to ask you to move," said the police officer.

"Why, of course!" The farmer lifted up the Cornish pasty to his lips. "I'll just need to eat this bad boy first, mind you."

Aled watched, as the man began munching away without any hesitation. Crumbs and meat flew out from his mouth as he spoke.

"Mmmm... delicious, these." Siôn's sheepdog leant across to lick away the scraps. "Oh, and don't worry about that little secret of ours. It won't go any further than me and Mott, over here. He wiped the grease from his mouth and pointed to *The Plas Coch Hotel* pub. "Just been meeting a few of the boys for a catch up. Just the one pint, of course!" He looked around and turned back to the police officer. "You're not thinking of breathalysing me or anything, are you?"

Aled let out a sigh. "I guess you seem like an honest individual."

"Good on you, Ali-lad! Always knew you were a top bloke." He gave the man a playful thump on the shoulder. "Hey, remember those dead arms I used to give you in school? Good times, eh?"

Aled straightened his collar. "Sure were. Now, about your *Land Rover*. I really need to ask you to move it."

"Never mind about that!" Siôn cried. "You need to get back to work. Crime doesn't fight itself, does it?"

"Siôn Puw!"

The farmer jumped at the sound of a second voice coming from the other side of his driver window. "Mrs Griffiths…"

The police officer turned to see that the teacher was now standing right beside him.

"You should be absolutely ashamed of yourself!" Nesta cried. "What would your mother think of you right now?"

Siôn struggled to get his words out through the crumbs in his mouth. "Well, I —"

"You're going to move this vehicle right this instant! Or Officer Parry, here, is going to remove you by force! Is that clear?"

The farmer continued to stutter, something he hadn't experienced since his school days.

"Or maybe you want to continue this conversation down at the station?" Nesta asked.

Siôn looked back at his former teacher with wide eyes. "Uh, no, Mrs Griffiths. That won't be necessary..." The man fired up his *Land Rover*. "Apologies for the inconvenience, officer."

Aled looked on in disbelief, as the vehicle pulled away at breakneck speed. Nesta stood beside him on the pavement shaking her head. "Some people have no respect for the law," she said.

The embarrassed police officer nodded at her and began walking back to his car. Nesta followed after him at a steady pace. "How's everything going?" she asked.

"Same old," said Aled. "Nothing new to report."

"Any news on the Dafydd Thomas case?"

The police officer paused once they had reached the police car. "Now, come on, Nesta. Even if there was, you know I couldn't tell you."

"Of course," said the teacher. "Absolutely. Have they found any leads?"

Aled sighed and realised that she wasn't going to leave him alone until he gave her something. "Look, all I can tell you is that another car's been spotted."

"Another car?"

"Dai Green spotted two vehicles down by the lake the night Dafydd was killed. He was walking his dog. One car was Dafydd's, and the other an unknown. That's all I can say. Nothing else!"

"Dai Green, you say?"

Aled slapped his own mouth. "Damn it, I shouldn't have said the name."

Nesta placed a hand on his shoulder. "Don't you worry, officer." She smiled. "I will keep this piece of information strictly confidential."

∽

THE LIBRARY at *Bala Secondary School* had been refurbished since Nesta's last tenure, and she was still struggling to navigate the various new bookshelves. Something about a wall of books gave her an overwhelming sense of excitement. Unlike the material objects of a shop, these bundles of paper could provide her an immediate portal into another world, and they were all at her fingertips. No plane ticket or holiday package could ever compare, and all she needed was a free hour and a cup of tea.

Browsing the shelves of the school library, Nesta was looking for one book in particular, and, after searching through a genre that was still very alien to her, she was struggling to complete her mission.

"Ah," said Emma, the librarian at the front desk, "that one's an early edition. We have the more recent ones in stock now." The woman lifted up Nesta's battered copy of *In Wolf's Clothing* and scurried off to find what she was looking for. When she returned, the sight of the cover in the librarian's hand sent the teacher into a panicked frenzy.

"Are you sure this is the right book?" Nesta asked, staring at the image of a shirtless man with a chiselled torso.

Emma nodded. "This is the second book in the *Dark Waters Academy* series." She took a quick glance at the handsome looking man and raised her eyebrow. "The latest editions really have made an effort with the covers, don't you think?"

Nesta took the book from her and hid it under her arms as

fast as possible, glancing over her shoulder to make sure nobody else had seen it. The male model featured on the cover was nothing like how she had pictured the main character at all. The character's in *her* head would never spend *that* much time at the gym, and she much preferred for some things to be left to the imagination.

"Enjoy," said Emma with a knowing smile.

The teacher blushed and struggled to work out which direction to walk in next. Fortunately, she didn't have to wonder for too long. If there was anything more shocking than the cover of her latest book, it was the sight of a certain pupil in the corner of the library. She headed over to him and wanted to poke the young man to check that he was real.

"Well, I never." The embarrassed teenager looked up at her. "Darren Price in a library… now I've seen everything."

"This isn't a good time," said Darren, peering over her shoulder. "Can we talk later?"

Nesta tried not to look offended. "I'm not embarrassing you, am I?" The teacher took a seat next to him. "I'll have you know I'm as cool as the next cucumber." She noticed him staring across the room again and saw Darren's fellow pupil, Lowri Meredydd, sitting in the opposite corner of the library. The young woman appeared to be deep into a study session. "Ah, I see. Doing some extra studying, are we?"

The young man cringed. "I don't know what you're talking about."

"Have you actually spoken to her yet?" Nesta asked. "Communication helps, you know."

"Okay, stop," Darren snapped. "I'm here to read."

"Of course you are." The teacher lifted up his book to look at the cover: *Evil Under The Sun* by Agatha Christie. "Ah, a good choice. Nothing like a little holiday to Devon, eh? Not very romantic though."

Darren frowned at her last sentence. "Don't you have exam papers to mark or something?"

Nesta shook her head. "I'm free as a bird. I don't have a lesson until two-thirty." She sat back in her chair as though it were a deck chair and exposed the cover of her book. The sound of the teenager's snorting laughter made her jolt back up again.

Darren snatched her reading material, waved it around and let out a giant wolf whistle.

"Yes, alright." Nesta tried to grab it back, but the young man was keeping it at arm's length whilst reading the blurb. "Believe it or not, I do have a pulse, you know? I might be old enough to be your grandmother, but even at our age, we still like —"

"*Please*," Darren insisted. "Don't say anymore." Suddenly, his amusement was quashed by the thought of his teacher getting too excited. "I don't want to know."

They both sat in silence for a while, until Nesta let out a loud yawn. Darren turned to her with a frown.

"Sorry," she said. "I always get sleepy at this time of the day."

"Maybe you should go and take a nap," said the teenager, trying to find his place again.

"I don't take naps," Nesta snapped. "Thank you very much! I'll nap when I'm dead." Her last word made Darren as uncomfortable as she had hoped, and it caused her to smile. "Talking of death..." She looked around and lowered her voice. "I discovered a very interesting new development this afternoon about the Dafydd Thomas case."

Darren lowered his book. She had his full attention now. "You *did*?"

Nesta nodded. "Turns out there was a second car spotted down by the lake."

The teenager's face lit up. "What make was it?"

"I've yet to find out," said Nesta. "But it sounds like Dafydd was meeting someone before he died."

"So that means he definitely knew the person who killed him," said Darren.

"It would seem so."

The two sleuths went quiet again, their minds spinning like a pair of spider webs.

"You still think it was a teacher?" Darren asked.

His question startled the woman. "Be careful what you say, boy!" she whispered. "We're in a school, for goodness sake."

"But you think it's likely?"

"It's possible," said Nesta. "But Dafydd's love life has also become quite complicated."

"So, it was a lover?"

The teacher crossed her arms and sighed. "I don't know why you're asking me these things as if I'm going to miraculously give you the actual solution. We're not at the end of an Agatha Christie book."

Darren shook his head in frustration. He would have given anything to find out the answer. "Do we know the *colour* of the second car?" he asked.

"No," said Nesta. She turned to him with a smile. "But I know someone who *does*."

Their conversation was suddenly interrupted by some movement on the other side of the room. "Quick!" Nesta whispered. "She's coming! Now's your chance."

The confused teenager watched Nesta stand up and realised that Lowri Meredydd was heading in their direction. "What are you doing?" he asked. His body began to tremble and his mind raced. "Don't you dare say anything!"

The teacher ignored his protests and greeted the young woman as she was about to head past. "Lowri!"

Darren felt his stomach begin to churn. He wanted, desperately, to grab hold of the teacher and pull her away.

"Mrs Griffiths," said Lowri. "That's a funny coincidence. I was just reading the rest of *An Inspector Calls*."

"Were you *really*?" asked Nesta. "I'm pleased to see at least *some* students take the initiative. Good for you."

Lowri shrugged. "I just really liked the story and had to find out the ending. It was so haunting!"

"I tell you who loves a good twist or two," Nesta said, pointing to a nervous Darren. "It's *this* young gentleman."

"Oh," said Lowri. She raised up her hand. "Hey, Darren."

The sound of his own name coming out of the young woman's mouth made him want to clutch his chest and keel over.

Nesta waited for Darren to respond, but the young man seemed to have lost his tongue. "Anyway," she said. "I'll leave you youngsters to it."

Once they were alone, the two awkward teenagers just stared at each other.

"So," said Lowri. "You like mystery books?"

Darren stared at her like a deer in the headlights and tried to play it cool. "Oh, yeah, sure. They're, like, awesome. Really awesome." In a burst of over-enthusiasm, he swung his arms around in a bid to find his book. Having dropped his Agatha Christie paperback down the back of the chair, he realised that another book was still lying on his lap.

"What's this?" asked Lowri. She reached across and picked up the novel.

Darren's throat went dry and his face turned a bright shade of red, as he saw her lift up Nesta's copy of the *Dark Waters Academy* sequel.

Lowri giggled at the sight of a half-naked man on the cover. "Wow," she said. "Well, I guess we all have our favourite genres."

"Oh," said Darren. "No, I can explain that."

Unfortunately, there was little time for the young man to

elaborate, as they were interrupted by the sound of a loud ringing noise.

"Saved by the bell," said Lowri with a cheeky wink. She bid Darren a farewell and left him to gaze down at the chiselled cover model staring back at him.

CHAPTER 20

Dai Green was like clockwork when it came to his walks: one at six o'clock in the morning, and the other at seven o'clock at night. It was a routine that he had kept since his Newfoundland, Sweep, was a small puppy. Living so close to a lake had been a blessing for the large dog, who loved nothing better than to soak his enormous, black coat in the waters of Llyn Tegid.

For the retired local photographer, who still did the occasional passport photo when required, his daily walks were a time for reflection, a moment where everything in the world seemed to stop.

Despite the same route, there was always something new to see every time he left the house, and, with the variety of seasons and weather, the view was never exactly the same each day. If he was lucky, Dai might have spotted a new breed of bird or come face to face with an unsuspecting otter, and, every once and a while, he might even have witnessed the early stages of a murder.

"Nesta?" he asked, as a figure approached him in the distance. "Fancy seeing you here."

"Yes," said Nesta. "Fancy that."

Her Jack Russell Hari was initially intimidated by the enormous Newfoundland, but it didn't stop him barking as though he wasn't a fraction of Sweep's size. Eventually, after giving each other a quick sniff, the two began playing and circling each other, until they ran off towards the lake.

"I'm surprised we don't bump into each other more often," said Dai. "Seeing as we walk the same route."

"You're too much of an early bird," said Nesta.

Dai Green was a few years older than Nesta and had grown up in the little village of Llanuwchllyn on the other side of the lake. She still remembered Dai from secondary school and was pleased to see that the man was still as handsome as he had been in his youth. Like her, Dai had also lost his lifelong partner to the cruel hands of fate and continued to live alone on the outskirts of the town.

They both gazed out at the calm water and clear sky.

"It never gets old, does it?"

Nesta turned to the man and smiled. "Unlike us, you mean?"

Dai laughed. "Time *does* fly. I don't know what happened to the last decade, but it feels like I've lost it somewhere underneath the sofa. "It feels like only yesterday I was in my twenties. Although, my body would disagree."

"You look fit and healthy to me," said Nesta. The man tried not to blush.

"How are the children?" asked Dai.

Nesta scoffed. "They're not children anymore. Erin lives in Mold and is just as much of a handful as she was as a teenager. And Bryn, who lives up in Edinburgh, has just told me that he's now moving to Australia with my first grandchild."

"Australia?" Dai slapped his forehead. "Why on earth would he want to go all the way to the other side of the world?"

"His wife's Australian."

"Ah. I see. Say no more."

"Don't get me wrong," said Nesta. "I love my daughter-in-law. But I will never forgive her for taking my firstborn to a different continent."

"Love can have that effect on people," said Dai. "It can take us to the ends of the earth."

The woman beside him turned to admire his face again. He had aged very well indeed and possessed a peacefulness that she almost envied. Perhaps it was all that bird-watching, she thought. "How are *you* keeping, Dai?"

"I'm still going." Dai chuckled. "That's the main thing."

"Well," said Nesta. "You can't say that for a lot of things in this town. I'm telling you now, if they close the chip shop, I'm leaving." She was struck by a sudden memory. "Remember when the Neuadd Buddug was still a cinema?"

Dai smiled and nodded. "Of course. I was the projectionist."

"I *know* you were. You've worn a lot of hats in your time, Dai Green, but that one was most appreciated."

"I loved that job," said Dai. "We only had three screenings a week, but people couldn't get enough of it."

Nesta couldn't agree more. "I used to drive past just to see what the poster was for the following week. It was so exciting when you saw the next release. And the intervals! God, I used to love those intervals. You'd come out for your ice cream and it would be a mad scramble."

"I needed those intervals just to recover from changing the reels!" Dai chuckled. "You should have seen how many we had for *Titanic*. It almost killed me!"

"Ah, Titanic..." Nesta could still picture being surrounded by all of her school pupils. "Yes, people were bawling their eyes out after that one. So was I. But not for that silly couple on a floating door. I cried for that poor elderly couple who stayed behind in their beds. Gosh, that really broke my heart even as a younger woman."

They watched their dogs jumping around together in the shallow water.

"Sorry," said Dai. "I feel like I brought the mood down by bringing up *Titanic*."

"Not to worry," said Nesta. "I started it by talking about things that have died away." She turned around and saw the area where Dafydd Thomas' car had been parked. "Speaking of which, it's terrible what happened down here recently."

Dai gave her a confused frown and saw the hollowness in her face. "Oh, right. Yes. I couldn't believe it when I heard. If only I'd —" The man paused and had a change of heart. "Ah, never mind."

"What is it?" Nesta asked.

"Well," said Dai. "I was walking Sweep down here the evening it happened, you see. I saw what turned out to be Dafydd Thomas' car over in the distance. I was walking right over there —" He pointed towards the weeds over in the far distance by the shore. "I was late that night. I had a meeting over at the town hall, and the sun had gone down by the time I got out here. There's nobody around normally at that time of the day, but I remember seeing this sportscar pulling up to park. Then, shortly afterwards, there was another car."

"Do you remember the make?" asked Nesta.

"It was a blue *Renault Clio*. I used to have a *Clio*, see. When I finally reported what I saw to the police, it turned out that the sportscar belonged to Dafydd."

"Did you see who was driving the *blue* car?"

Dai shook his head. "It was too dark to see who was inside either of them. And I left before they got out of their cars." The man scratched his chin. "I never in a million years would have thought someone was about to be killed. The whole thing just makes my skin crawl."

"We've done it again," said Nesta. The fellow dog walker turned to see her warm smile. "Let's talk about something nice again. Like the movies."

Dai smiled back. They had indeed verged off into a gloomy conversation about death and tragedy. He'd had enough of that in his life already and was more than willing to change the subject. "Well," he said, "I *have* always been a bit of a film buff."

"Is that right?" Nesta asked. "I wouldn't say I'm quite as knowledgeable about the silver screen as I am about books and literature, but I do love a good movie night. Nothing like a bit of popcorn and a good film."

"Tell me about it!" Dai's eyes were wild with excitement. He didn't often get to discuss one of his favourite subjects with someone (or at least with someone who was willing to listen), and the man had to contain himself. "You know, during the nineties, when I was still living in Llanuwchllyn, I used to walk the entire length of this lake to rent a film. My wife used to have the car on Fridays, you see." He pointed towards the village on the far side of this three-and-a-half-mile stretch of water (not that any of them could see it without a telescope). Dai could tell she was impressed. "Oh, yes! I'm serious! I would follow that little railway line all the way into town to *Derwen Stores*."

"*Derwen Stores...*" The name of her favourite local shop sent a rush of nostalgia through Nesta's bones. "Best sweets in Bala."

Dai nodded. "Then, I'd take my video tape and walk all the way back again."

Nesta laughed. "You were like Mary Jones and her bible!"

"Those were the days," said Dai. "Back then, you had to *earn* your entertainment. Now, people have anything they want on their *Flixnet*. But I can tell you now, they didn't have the joy I felt picking out that video tape and bringing it home."

"Or the blisters," said Nesta, pointing to his feet.

The man laughed in agreement and checked his watch. "I should better get Sweep home. It takes me half an hour just to get his coat dry." The Newfoundland was still leaping around in the water whilst showing off to the bemused Jack Russell.

Nesta tried to conceal her disappointment at his imminent departure. "We should do this more often," she said.

Dai turned around to see her warm gaze. "Yes. Yes, we should."

The woman in front of him tried desperately to force out a suggestion, but her nerves got the better of her. Come on, she said to herself — *ask him*. By the time she had plucked up the courage to propose a coffee, the man had begun walking away towards his dog. "You daft woman," she muttered under her breath.

"Take care of yourself, Nesta!" Dai called.

The teacher gave him a little wave. "You too, Dai."

CHAPTER 21

"Why are you going *this* way?" Darren asked whilst holding on for dear life in the passenger seat of his driver's car.

"Do you know how many times I've driven to Wrexham in my life?" Nesta asked back, taking her eyes off the road for a moment. "I've been going there since before you were born. And this is always the way I go."

The teenager was beginning to regret his decision to take Nesta up on her offer. He had been standing at an empty bus stop when she drove past, and, as fate would have it, they were heading in the same direction.

Darren had been looking forward to seeing his favourite heavy metal band in concert and had been willing to take a number of buses to get there. He would have done anything to make the gig, except, it had turned out, put his life on the line in Nesta's *Citroën*.

"There's a sharp turn coming up," he said to the frustration of his driver.

"I'm sorry," said Nesta. "I didn't realise that you'd passed your test at such a young age." The jolt as she turned the steering wheel caused her passenger to brace himself. "Will you *please* relax? This is safer than one of your mosh pits."

Nesta had been setting out to buy her first mobile phone when she came across the lonely figure standing beside the bus stop. Her first instinct had been to try Mold, but she also realised that Wrexham was the same amount of travel time, so a change in destination was perfectly reasonable.

Darren had also offered to help out with the new mobile phone, something she had never envisioned purchasing until the news of her son's move to Australia. If she was to ever see her grandchild's face again over the next few years, then the ability to make video calls was vital, and even *she* had to turn to the darkside.

"How's Lowri?" she asked, as they entered the village of Coedpoeth.

The teenager saw her playful gaze and scrunched up his arms with a pout. "You tell me."

"I thought you two were getting close," said Nesta.

"That's only because we sit next to each other in English class," Darren snapped. "Besides, she's not interested in someone like me."

"What makes you think that?" She waited for a response, but her passenger remained quiet. "You'll never know if you don't ask." Nesta stared out through her windscreen at the winding road. "Sometimes, the actions people take at your age stay with them forever. Or, in some cases, the actions we *don't* take. I've always regretted not asking a young man called Dewi Pritchard out to the graduation party."

Darren sat up in his seat. "You were in love with Mr Pritchard?"

Nesta wanted to bury her head in the glove compartment. For a split second, she had completely forgotten that Dewi Pritchard was now the woodwork teacher. "I wasn't in *love* with him," she snapped. "It was just a little crush, that's all. But my point is that you take the opportunities when they're presented to you. Or it'll haunt you forever."

"You're haunted by not asking out Mr Pritchard?" Darren asked and roared with laughter.

"No!" Nesta cried. "I didn't mean —" She sighed. "Never mind. Just keep doing what you're doing. Bury your head in the sand and see how far that gets you."

"If you must know," said Darren. "I *have* asked Lowri out."

The car went silent. "You *did*?"

Her deflated passenger nodded. "I asked her out to the concert. I'd even bought two tickets. She said no."

"Oh," said Nesta, feeling slightly guilty for asking. "I'm sorry to hear that."

Darren shrugged. "It's no big deal. She also said that she hated heavy metal music. So that would never have worked."

"I guess not." They both sat in silence for another mile, until Nesta had an idea. "Hey! I know what we need!" The driver reached across and pushed a cassette tape into the mouth of the car radio. "A little bit of Engelbert."

The teenager listened in horror, as the song "Release Me," by Engelbert Humperdinck blasted out through the speakers.

"Who did you say this was?" he asked. "Engel — what?"

"Engelbert Humperdinck," said Nesta.

"Okay," Darren muttered. "Now I *know* you're making that up." He clutched his ears as it reached the chorus. "Can we turn it down a bit?"

"*What*?!"

"It's too loud!"

The teenager's voice didn't seem to be getting through to his driver's hearing aids, and he reached across to turn down the volume.

Nesta huffed. "I thought you heavy metal people liked your music loud?"

"Not *that* loud," said Darren, rubbing the inside of his ears. "You must be deaf."

"I'm probably not that far off," said Nesta.

After going on to discuss Dai Green's visual description of the second car down by the lake, they drove into the *Island Green* car park in Wrexham town centre.

"Can you think of anyone who drives a blue *Renault Clio*?" Darren asked.

His driver shook her head. "Nobody I know."

"So that doesn't help us much." Darren breathed a sigh of relief, as she turned the engine off. He had made it in one piece, and all he had to do now was brave the mobile phone shop with a technophobic woman who thought 4G was an unusual bra size.

"Right," said Nesta. "Where do we start?"

The teenager shrugged. "I don't know. There's a *Currys* just around the corner."

His driver rubbed her hands with delight. "Excellent idea! I'm absolutely starving."

~

"Are you *sure* this is the place?"

The *Citroën* was now parked up outside a rundown building.

Darren peered through the windscreen and saw a queue of men and women dressed in an excessive amount of leather and denim. "Definitely."

The teenager thanked his driver and opened up his passenger door.

"I'll wait here then, shall I?" Nesta asked.

Her passenger froze. "Hey?"

"I'll wait until the concert's finished and give you a lift home." She lifted up her latest paperback. "I'm very good at killing time."

A surprised Darren shook his head. "You don't need to drive me home as well. I'll find my way back."

"At that time of night?" his driver asked. "There's no way you can walk *that* far. And there won't be any buses that late."

The young man knew that she raised a good point, but it didn't stop him from feeling guilty. "I can't let you sit in the car and wait for me. You're not my mam!"

Nesta was struck with a sudden idea. "I know — I'll come with you!"

Darren scoffed. "You want to join me for a heavy metal concert?"

"Why not?" the teacher asked. "You said you have two tickets."

"Yeah, but —" He gave it some thought before immediately realising that it was an absolutely terrible idea. "No," he said, slicing his hands in the air. "No way! There's no way in a million years I'm going to watch Deathdemons with a person old enough to be my grandmother. It's not happening."

Moments later, Darren and Nesta had both joined the long queue of heavy metal fans.

"You know how loud it's going to be in there?" the teenager asked. "My ears were ringing after the last concert."

Nesta tapped her ear. "Doesn't bother me. I'll just turn off my hearing aids."

Darren shook his head and continued to sulk. "Well, you're going to be too hot in that fleece."

"It's freezing out here," said the teacher, shivering away.

"It might be cold now, but, by the time you get inside with all those people, you'll be sweating. I promise you."

"Not even a sauna can make me sweat these days," Nesta muttered. She looked at the enormous haircut of the person in front of her, which resembled a large, green spike that could be seen for miles. "I'm more worried about inhaling all of the hairspray fumes."

Once they had entered the main hall, they were faced with even more people with flamboyant hair and studded outfits. The atmosphere was buzzing with excitement, as the crowd waited in anticipation for the first act.

Nesta and Darren weaved their way through the clusters of heavy metal fans, trying to get closer to the stage.

"Excuse me, thank you — pardon me, yes — sorry..."

Nesta's loud apologies made the teenager cringe, until they finally reached front.

"Hey! Mrs Griffiths!"

The teacher turned around to see a man with an enormous beard and a bald head.

"It's me," the man cried. "Seimon!"

"*Seimon*? Seimon Dobson?" Nesta stared at her former pupil's excited face. He was a far cry from the shy young man that she remembered in her English class.

"I never knew you were a metal-head!"

"Well," said Nesta. "I'm never opposed to trying new things. I did yoga the other day."

"You're going to love it," said Seimon. "I'm the venue's sound engineer. Best job in the world!"

His old teacher tried to appear impressed. She would have hardly used the word "venue" for a concrete building with no windows or a lack of plumbing but admired the man's enthusiasm. "Good for you."

The crowd was silenced by an explosion of noise from the enormous speakers on either side of the stage. Suddenly, an orchestral intro caused Nesta's ears to prick up. She listened to what sounded like a familiar segment from the opera *Requiem* and raised her arms in the air.

"It's Donizetti!" The elated woman turned to a confused Darren and shook him. "They're paying Donizetti!"

After another minute of dramatic music, the piece was cut short by a roar of electric guitars, as a group of musicians with long hair and bundles of energy took to the stage whilst banging their heads.

Nesta was struck by her first proper dose of hardcore heavy metal music and witnessed a sea of people starting to bob their heads in unison.

"Goodness," she said. "I don't remember *this* bit in *Requiem*."

Darren seemed to be as enthusiastic as everyone else around her, and, had she not been wearing her favourite heels, she would have tried to blend in with the relentless jumping. Just as she was getting tempted to remove her fleece, Nesta felt something vibrating in her pocket and initially wanted to call an ambulance. She pulled the unfamiliar object out into the open and saw that her new mobile phone was receiving its first call.

"Oh!" she cried, trying to get Darren's attention. "It's working! It's *working*!"

In a burst of excitement she inadvertently answered the incoming video call and saw her son's confused face in the middle of the screen.

"Bryn!" Nesta called out. "Bryn! I can see you!"

Her son squinted his eyes. "Mam?! Where are you?" Nesta lifted up the phone into the air to reveal a large crowd of head-banging heavy metal fans. The man gave his mother a concerned look, as she held the phone up to her ear as though it were a landline.

"I can't hear you, Bryn! You'll have to speak up!"

CHAPTER 22

A bleary-eyed Nesta shoved an extra spoonful of coffee into her mug and poured the hot water. She was normally a tea-drinker, but desperate times had required desperate measures. Caffeine was her only hope now, especially if she was going to survive a geography lesson with Year Nine. The subject had never been her strongpoint in the first place, having barely travelled further than the end of the A55.

The rock concert the night before had very much taken its toll, and she could still hear a faint ringing noise that seemed to follow her everywhere.

"Careful," said a voice behind her. "That coffee belongs to Berwyn Lewis. He'll go ballistic."

Nesta turned around to find Gwen Williams clutching her own mug. The receptionist looked at her as if she were a dead woman walking.

"Berwyn brings his own coffee to school?" Nesta asked with disgust.

Gwen nodded. "He's very particular about how he makes it.

Oh, and it's not instant coffee, either." She pointed at the solid lumps floating in Nesta's mug. "He uses a French press."

The older woman scoffed and chucked her drink in the sink. "It's coffee — not a science experiment. You don't need a plunger."

"Could have been worse," said Gwen. "You could have used his mug."

Nesta huffed. "You think I'm scared of the likes of Berwyn Lewis in the mood I'm in today?" She pictured grabbing the skinny maths teacher by the scruff of the neck and shaking him around like a rag doll.

Gwen saw the bags under her eyes and pouted. "Rough night?"

"Something like that," said Nesta, foraging through the cupboard for the instant coffee.

"I know the feeling," said the receptionist. "I never know when to stop when I'm on the gin. I've still got blisters from Saturday night at *The Goat*. Cocktails, karaoke and a dancefloor — my three worst vices. So, what was your poison last night?"

"Heavy metal," said Nesta.

Her answer almost left the younger woman speechless. "Oh. That sounds... nice."

"Is that Berwyn Lewis' coffee?" asked Dewi Pritchard on his way past the sink. "Christ, you're brave, Nesta."

The supply teacher gave him a dirty look, as he headed out of the room.

"Berwyn Lewis..." Gwen muttered with a shudder, nursing her mug of hot tea. "Now *there's* a psychopath if ever I saw one. I mean, who brings their own milk and butter everyday?" Her mouth formed a wicked grin. "Hey! Do you think he was the one who killed Dafydd Thomas?"

Nesta shook her head and was disappointed to find that someone had put an empty milk carton back in the fridge. "Now,

now, Gwen. Be nice. The man clearly has an obsessive-compulsive disorder of some kind. It's no laughing matter."

The receptionist was disappointed by her lack of amusement, but she wasn't deterred. "It's always the oddballs. I suppose anyone who teaches a subject like maths is going to be a bit strange. Then there's the argument..."

The teacher slurped her black tea and turned to her. "*Argument?*"

Gwen gave her an excited grin. "I saw those two at each other's throats only a few weeks ago. I could see the whole thing from my desk. They were out in the car park. Should have got some popcorn."

"Who?"

"Dafydd and Berwyn."

～

BERWYN LEWIS CURSED at his whiteboard and wiped away an entire formula. He hated it when his writing got smudged and, as a left-handed individual, had suffered his entire life. The maths teacher knew that his pupils wouldn't care, but *he* did. There was still another fifteen minutes until his next class, and he was adamant that the entire list of problems would be down in time.

His pupils had always been frustrated by the man's tendency to spend more time writing and solving the problems himself rather than actually explaining the methods in the first place. Berwyn was a very good mathematician, but his teaching skills left a lot to be desired. His main problem was empathy. As a natural wizard of numbers, he couldn't possibly understand how a person could not come to these conclusions themselves. After all, it was perfectly obvious.

On his third attempt to rewrite the next formula, he could

smell a familiar brand of perfume. "Nesta Griffiths," he said without turning around.

"Hello, Berwyn. You missed a bit." Nesta watched the startled man squint at his whiteboard, until he turned to find her smirking face. "Sorry," she said. "I wouldn't know the difference between a dirty mark and a square root."

Berwyn humoured her with a nod. "I'm sorry, Nesta. This really isn't a good time."

The woman admired his spotless desk and wished that hers had come close to such organisation. His parallel positioning of the ruler and pens were a particularly nice touch. But, sometimes, life was too short. "That's a shame," she said. "I was hoping you could help me to solve this problem I have."

Nesta knew the man too well and was pleased to get his full attention.

"What *sort* of problem?" he asked, placing the lid back on his marker.

"Oh, you know." She began pacing around the empty desks. "The type of conundrum that only a keen mind like yourself could hope to decipher. It's been driving me crazy."

"Go on," said Berwyn, heading back to his desk.

"Well," Nesta continued. "Suppose you take a man that not many people seem to like, and, the next minute, he disappears — vanishes into thin air. Where would you begin to work out what happened?"

The disappointed maths teacher sighed. He was hoping for something a little more in his wheelhouse — like geometry or calculus. Instead, he was aware that the woman was toying with him, and he decided to indulge her anyway.

"It would depend," he said. "How did this person vanish?"

"I suppose *vanish* wasn't the best word." Nesta sat herself down on one of the desks. "Let's go with — *murdered* — in cold blood."

Berwyn swallowed a hard gulp. "Is there any other kind?"

"The person was left lying beside a lake after having had his head battered and nobody knows how he got there," Nesta continued. "It's quite the lateral puzzle, don't you think?"

The maths teacher took his time to respond and deliberated on the details. "I can presume who you might be talking about. But I'm afraid, like most deaths, there is nothing particularly remarkable about *this* particular incident. The man had far too much to drink, he slipped, hit his head on a rock. Tragic but probably nothing more than that."

"That's *some* rock," said Nesta.

Berwyn raised his hands. "People die from a sneeze. We're quite fragile creatures at times."

Nesta could see what Gwen had meant: the man came across as very cold in his demeanour, but she also knew that he possessed a very dry sense of humour — a poor one, but dry nonetheless. "You'd make such a comforting doctor, Berwyn."

The man smiled. It wasn't an action he did very often, and when he did, it was like his lips had to force the rest of his face to move. "Sorry to be so bleak. But *you're* the one who came in here talking about death."

"True," said Nesta. "I suppose we can both be very morbid." She stared at the formations on his whiteboard, which might as well have been random squiggles. "You really don't think he was killed? The police seem to think so, according to the papers."

"I try to avoid the news," said Berwyn. "It's often very negative and not conducive to a person's mental wellbeing."

Nesta chuckled. "That explains why you're always so overwhelmingly positive, Berwyn."

The maths teacher detected a hint of sarcasm and stretched out his lips again. "I try to keep an open mind and take in all of my information with a pinch of salt. Plus, my day-to-day is hard enough without worrying about the rest of the world."

His fellow teacher wasn't surprised. She could only imagine how exhausting it must have been to have such an obsessive mind like Berwyn Lewis. It was easy to imagine him spending a whole hour just arranging his shoes. His house must have been as pristine as his desk, she thought. "I can imagine you being very neat and tidy at home."

"Uh, yes, I suppose cleanliness is a big priority." The man seemed a little anxious at the thought of his housekeeping. "I try not to let it get out of hand. As I'm sure people are already aware, I can be a little compulsive sometimes. I used to be a lot worse."

"I wish I was half as organised," said Nesta. "I haven't even done the ironing since — well, I can't even remember!"

"I'm not quite as productive as you might think," said Berwyn. "I can spend hours doing menial tasks like scrubbing the bath or organising the cupboards. But there's no rhyme or reason to it. The bigger things can often get neglected. There's only so many hours in the day."

Nesta saw a sadness in him that she pitied, as though he was suffering from a cruel disease. Perhaps he didn't necessarily want to be organising his shoes, she realised, but that he had no choice. She turned her mind back to the case of Dafydd Thomas and was keen to use the man's logical brain to assist her. Nesta's own mind was far too burdened by emotion and preconceived ideas.

"Let us say that Dafydd Thomas was definitely murdered," she said. "Who would be top of your list?"

Berwyn laughed. "What a question. I barely knew the man. I wouldn't know where to start."

"Did you ever have any confrontation with him yourself?" Nesta asked. She knew Berwyn Lewis was many things but doubted that he was a liar. He was often known for his bluntness and seemed to live his life like an open book.

"Actually," he said, "there *was* this one argument we had." The man almost seemed too embarrassed to continue. "It was in the school car park, shortly after he purchased his *Maserati*." The woman in front of him listened with keen interest. "As you know, we teachers who drive to school have our designated parking spots. It's an unspoken rule, but we've always stuck to it. My spot has always been right outside the front entrance. It's a perk of having worked here for so long."

Nesta was aware of the unofficial lines that he spoke of. Personally, she had never needed to drive to school. But the rule was clear: stick to your own parking space.

"One day," Berwyn continued, "I came to work, and there it was — Dafydd's new *Maserati*. It was parked in my space. I almost had a panic attack."

"I imagine he wanted to show off his new toy," said Nesta. "Your spot was prime retail for that. What did you do?"

"After a few breathing exercises, I parked my car behind his and tried to find him. I searched everywhere, and, by the time I got back, he was standing next to my car — as if I was obstructing *him*!" The anger in his voice was clear. "I just snapped. I began shouting at him, and he accused me of being crazy. He said everyone thought I was crazy and told me to go park somewhere else. Eventually, I moved my car to a space across the street from the school. I sat there for so long to calm down that I was late for my first lesson. I've never been late for a lesson!" His hands began to shake. "That really was the day from hell."

Nesta felt another surge of pity. She was beginning to realise that everything in Berwyn Lewis' world was under a microscope. His life was a small bubble of existence with its own rules and regulations.

"I'm sorry you had to experience that," she said.

Berwyn still seemed embarrassed. He was not an emotional

person but that incident in the car park had clearly shaken him up. "It's all very trivial really," he said. "I'm aware of that."

The school bell broke their momentary silence, and Nesta stood up from the desk. She was about to leave the man to his formulas, when she paused to ask a final question: "Can I ask you something, Berwyn?" The man nodded. "Remind me — what type of car do you drive?"

CHAPTER 23

The small cul-de-sac known as Mawnog Fach was a quiet part of town. Each bungalow was neatly spaced apart, and many of the occupants had lived there all of their lives. Located on the outskirts of Bala, it was not a street that Nesta normally had the excuse to visit.

When she reached a blue door with a house name, Cysgod Y Berwyn, there was already a figure in the frosted glass.

"What are you doing here?" Donna Lloyd asked, having swung her front door open in an aggressive manner.

"I've come to apologise," said Nesta. She raised her arms and waved an imaginary white flag. "I didn't mean to upset you the other day. I know you're going through a lot."

Donna looked down at the box of luxurious biscuits in Nesta's hand and rolled her eyes. She headed back inside, leaving the door wide open. "Come on, then."

Nesta entered the small living room to find the television blazing with a daytime chat show and a takeaway box still lying there from the night before. "I'm not a charity case, you know. I don't want you thinking of me as this helpless fiancée, wallowing in grief."

"I never thought anything of the sort," said the older woman, trying to find an empty spot amongst all the washing.

Her host stood in front of a large mirror which made the room appear larger than it really was. "I did feel quite bad for snapping at you like that. It's been a weird few weeks."

"I've been teaching teenagers my whole career," said Nesta. "I've heard a lot worse."

Donna smiled. "I'm sure you have."

"I won't stay long. I'm on a lunch break."

The young woman slumped down onto the sofa. "Fair enough. It's nice to have a visitor. I never thought moving back to my hometown would be so lonely."

"What about your parents?" asked Nesta.

"They're separated nowadays," said Donna. "They left Bala shortly after I moved away to university. All my friends have either moved themselves or they're married with children. When we first moved back up, I was expecting to see everyone from school, walking around town like it was fifteen years ago. But so much has changed."

"You're not wrong there," said the teacher. "It's harder to see the changes when you've never left, but they're still there. The problem is that you only notice them at the last minute. One day, it just hits you like a delayed reaction."

Donna stared at her. "I assume you're retired now?"

"Sort of." Nesta chuckled. "I recently came out of retirement to do some supply teaching — like an old boxer, lacing back up my gloves." She paused to reflect for a moment. "Actually, I could probably do with some boxing gloves the way that school is at the moment."

"Is that funny Mr Mellon still around?" Donna asked.

"No, he's long gone. But there's a few of the old guard still around, hanging on for dear life."

The young woman nodded. "I think Dafydd found it quite a

strange being back there. The whole thing gave him a bit of a midlife crisis."

"Is that where the *Maserati* came in?"

Donna groaned. "Don't get me started on that thing. He was a little reckless when it came to finances. Just because everything was cheaper here than it was down south, he acted like we'd won the lottery. Plus, he was trying to compete with Johnny Glyn." She lifted up the luxury box of biscuits. "Do you mind if we —"

"I bought them for *you*," said her guest. The young woman ripped open the box and began helping herself.

Nesta could sense that she was a little on edge. "Do you remember what Dafydd was like on the last day you saw him?" she asked.

Donna finished her mouthful. "Same as he always was — steaming drunk." The other woman could hear the contemptuous tone in her voice. "He'd just come back from the pub with a black eye."

"This was the night he died?" Nesta asked, sitting forward in her seat.

Her host nodded after another biscuit. "We had a massive argument that evening. That wasn't unusual, either. We rowed a lot since we moved back. Like I said before, the move home didn't exactly make us happier. Things were pretty toxic."

Nesta struggled with what she wanted to talk about next and decided it was not worth breaking a young woman's heart when it no longer made any difference. "Did his behaviour change at all when you moved back? Was he a little more distant, like —"

"Like he was having an affair?"

Nesta went silent. She had hoped that Donna would never find out.

"Yes," Donna continued. "I knew about the affair. That little cockroach..." She clenched her fist and caused the biscuit in her hand to crumble. "He wasn't exactly careful about it. I found a load of messages one day on his phone. He was in the shower, and I wanted to scream the house down. Strangely enough, once he came out, I couldn't bring myself to confront him about it. I think a part of me was curious — curious to see how long he'd carry it on for — how far he would go to hide it. So I didn't say anything. All of a sudden, it became obvious — all the excuses, the lies... his strange behaviour suddenly made sense. So, I just waited for the right moment and carried on as normal. Looking at him made me sick, but I put up with it for as long as I could."

The older woman had been listening with a weary face. "That night before he died," she said. "The night you had your big argument. Is that when you told him you knew?"

Donna shook her head, and a tear streamed down her cheek. "That was just a meaningless argument. It only blew up because he was drunk. I came very close to telling him, though, but he stormed back out the house. I knew exactly where he was heading, so I followed him all the way to Trem Y Ffridd. The house was called Afon Enfawr. I parked up, further down the street. Watched him walk out of his car and head inside the house. He didn't even know I was watching." More tears started to trickle down her face. "I waited there, picturing myself walking into that house and catching them both in the act — watching their faces as they realised they'd been caught. But as the minutes went on, my whole body froze up. My hands were glued to the steering wheel. I couldn't bring myself to do it. I don't know why. I'd dreamt about bashing them both over the head with a frying pan and trashing the entire house. But I realised they were just fantasies. I felt like a pathetic fool."

"So what did you do?" asked Nesta, fearing the worst.

"I just turned the car back on and drove away," said Donna. "I parked up in the high street and just sat there, staring into space. Half an hour later, I saw Dafydd's car drive past and assumed he was heading back home. But that's the last time I saw it."

"And what time was this?"

Donna shrugged. "Seven? Eight, maybe? I don't really remember. But the sun had gone down, and I remember it being dark. When I got back to the house, Dafydd wasn't there. And he never came home."

Nesta climbed to her feet. She had heard everything that she needed to know but was far from satisfied. There were a few more visits that she had to make, a few more people that she needed to call in on. But, either way, Nesta realised, she was getting close. She could feel it in her bones: the jigsaw puzzle was starting to take shape.

CHAPTER 24

Dyfrig Thomas pounded his shovel against the stubborn soil. He sliced and slashed, again and again, until he was completely out of breath. Nothing in the world gave him that much satisfaction. The physical labour of preparing a new flower bed had always been a much needed release, and he needed that now more than ever.

After the amount of death in his life up until that point, he couldn't wait to bring a new lease of life into the world. Death was a very natural part of life, especially at his age: parents, friends, loved ones... none of them had been spared by that cold hand of fate.

Nobody had been more surprised than him that an activity like gardening was to be his saving grace. Just like life, the act of planting a seed and watching it grow was a journey with a beginning, middle and an end. Everything that blossomed would eventually perish, and there was nothing he could do about it.

"Don't you go doing your back in."

Dyfrig listened to the voice coming from the other side of his garden fence and nodded. "Nesta Griffiths..."

The retired head teacher looked up at his former staff member and felt transported back in time. Her face may have changed a little over the years, but he still recognised that burning fire in her eyes.

"I'm so sorry," Nesta said.

Her former boss took a moment to work out what she was referring to, and, in a heartbeat, his grief swelled back up again. Perhaps the gardening really *had* taken his mind off things for a brief moment.

"Is that why you came?"

Nesta decided to be honest. She knew the man could see straight through her. All those years of disciplining unruly young people turned a person into a human lie detector. "It wasn't, actually."

"That makes a change," said Dyfrig. "It's amazing how many people have visited me over the last few weeks because of... what happened. Most of them would never have darkened my door otherwise."

"I can't imagine what you're going through," said Nesta. "No parent should ever have to experience such a tragedy."

Dyfrig stuck his shovel down in the dirt and leant himself against its handle. "Tragedy's one word for it. But we all know our Dafydd wasn't run over by a bus." He stroked his enormous beard. "Somebody out there is responsible. And I'd like to bury them in this very front garden."

Nesta could see the pain and anger in his face — the thirst for revenge and a desire to seek it. "Is there anybody you know who would likely do such a thing?"

Her question surprised him. So far, all of his visitors had said very little except the usual stock responses that a person gave when offering their condolences. Dyfrig had simply let people's words pass by without a glimmer of interest. Nothing that anybody had said could help to numb the pain, but a genuine question involving his son's killer lit a fire within him.

"People are capable of terrible things," he said. "Even from a very early age. We both know that." The two retired teachers gave each other a knowing look. "But murder? That's a whole different beast."

"You might be aware that I recently came out of retirement," said Nesta.

Her old head teacher lifted up his curious face. "Is that right?" The man chuckled. "Couldn't adapt to civilian life, eh? I never could imagine a retired Nesta Griffiths. I can only imagine the trouble that you've been causing."

Nesta smiled. "It hasn't been easy twiddling my thumbs. So, I agreed to do some supply teaching."

Dyfrig scoffed. "You're a brave woman! We all remember those supply teachers. It was like throwing someone to the wolves."

"Not very much has changed," said Nesta. "But a lot has."

"I think Dafydd took a little while to settle in," said Dyfrig. "I always hoped he'd follow in my footsteps. I'd long given up that dream until he came back to Bala. You can imagine my surprise when that happened." He shook his head in despair. "As fate would have it, turns out he was safer living somewhere else." His voice began to break, and he forced himself to stand up straight. "It's why I'm adamant it was someone close to him."

"You mean —" Nesta struggled to find the right words. "The person who —"

"Yes," said Dyfrig. "The person who killed him." His silence was accompanied by some gentle birdsong. "They say it's always someone you know. I mean, the odds of it — all those years away, and then, suddenly, he's back in his hometown and something happens? It's ridiculous!" He lifted up the shovel and slammed it back down again. "They always say it's the partner.

But that doesn't make sense, either. Why leave it that long? After moving back home?"

"I spoke to Donna yesterday," said Nesta. "She's a bit of a wreck."

"She will be. She's as much a victim in all this as anyone. And the police don't seem to be getting anywhere."

Nesta made eye contact with him and stared him down. "I think this case is closer to being solved than you might think. Trust me."

Her old colleague saw the seriousness in her face and laughed. "Ah, Nesta. I wish I shared your optimism and faith in the law. I'm sure Morgan is sorely missed in that police station. Now *there* was a damn good police officer."

"He's sorely missed at home," said Nesta. Her own voice had decided to break this time. The widow couldn't quite understand why, but she suddenly had the urge to break down in tears. She had shed many tears over her husband's death, but why they would want to drop over Dyfrig Thomas' garden fence was a mystery she would never solve. Grief, it seemed, played strange tricks on a person.

"I never got to offer my condolences," said Dyfrig.

Nesta continued to stare down at the mound of earth beneath his feet. "Sometimes I still hear his voice. Most of the time, it's stupid things, like telling me to stop worrying. Or to stop buying the cheap chocolate digestives again. But, lately, his words have been more like a compass, guiding me through various problems, as if he's dropping me breadcrumbs." She saw Dyfrig's confused expression and shook her head. "It probably makes no sense to anyone else."

"If there's one thing that never dies," the man said with a shrug, "it's love." He let out a laugh. "It makes me sound like a hopeless romantic. Linda would have highly disagreed, God rest her soul." Dyfrig stretched out his arms and felt a muscle pull in his back. "Don't you ever wish you could go back in time, Nesta? Back to when everything was so much simpler."

"Back to when you could boss me around, you mean?"

The man chuckled. "I wouldn't have dared. You were one of my best teachers. You know why? Because you were a pain in my backside."

"That's only because all the other teachers were scared of you," said Nesta with an eye roll.

Dyfrig was almost flattered. "Yes, I suppose they probably were. Never could understand why. I was hardly a monster."

"Monster..." Nesta heard that voice in her head again. "Yes, *now* it makes sense," she muttered. The teacher felt a newfound sense of urgency and prepared to make her swift exit.

Dyfrig could tell that her mind was elsewhere and decided to continue his plowing session. "Send my regards to the old gang," he said.

The fellow veteran teacher acknowledged his request. She was about to head off, when Nesta paused and turned back around. "Actually," she said. "Do you mind if I ask you one last question?"

CHAPTER 25

Nesta made her way down the street of Trem Y Ffridd with a stomach full of butterflies. Her private investigation into the mystery of Dafydd Thomas had not been without its difficulties. In a town where most people knew her name, it had still not been easy to acquire the necessary information, and her questions had raised far more suspicion than they had clues. Sometimes, as her late husband would have preached, a person had to use their instinct — and if there was one thing driving Nesta Griffiths to that front door, it was her gut.

All roads in the little town of Bala had led to this: Afon Enfawr. The house name had been carved into a piece of Welsh slate and referred to the great Afon Dyfrdwy (or River Dee) which flowed as far as the English city of Chester.

Nesta took a deep breath of courage and gave the front door a solid *knock*. Within a matter of seconds the person she had expected to find was standing there in the open doorway.

"Nesta," said the homeowner. "What a nice surprise."

"Hello, Catrin."

The deputy head teacher was as warm and inviting as she

had been on every visit, but, on this occasion, the visitor was very uncomfortable.

"Sorry about the mess," said Catrin Jones, leading her guest into the small kitchen. "If I'd have known you were coming —"

"You don't need to clean for me," said Nesta, sitting herself down at the kitchen table. Her eyes fell on a paperback with the title: *Forbidden Fruit*. She picked up the book and heard the kettle begin to boil. "Ah, let me guess — another one of your dark romances?"

Catrin blushed. "You must think I've got a problem."

"On the contrary," her friend said. "I find the whole genre fascinating. Dark romance is a lot broader than I realised."

"Been doing some research, have we?" Catrin gave her a cheeky wink.

Nesta smiled back. "I did a bit of a deep dive on the subject. Our local librarian is very knowledgeable. Romance is not half as straightforward as it used to be."

"I think it's evolved a bit since the days of Jane Austen," said Catrin.

"Yes and no," said Nesta. "Jane Austen was quite ahead of her time in many ways. Some of the old tropes are still present, but now they're almost unrecognisable." She lifted up the book. "Take that series you introduced me to — turns out it's a popular sub-genre within another sub-genre. *Enemies to lovers*: a popular romance genre that would appear timeless. There's nothing new about two characters falling in love after initially hating each other. Even Jane was no stranger to *that* one. And take this series." The book was now the centre of attention again. "They call it *Bully Romance* — a sub-genre of *Enemies to Lovers* — where the main character is tormented by their bully, only for them to later engage in a passionate love affair. Now, throw in the supernatural element and you've got a mish-mash of genres that makes my head spin. Now you have a bully who's literally a monster or a demon but also incredibly handsome on the outside."

Catrin's mobile phone vibrated on the counter and almost startled her. She checked her message and placed it back down on the table. "I'm sorry," she said. "Can you just excuse me a minute? Hywel just needs me to check something on the car." The deputy headteacher rushed off and left her visitor alone in the kitchen.

Nesta could see the open messages on the phone and couldn't resist taking a look. Now that she had switched to the dark side of owning a mobile phone herself, she was competent enough to navigate the previous messages. One thread in particular caught her eye, and she knew her suspicions had been right. Below the name Dafydd were a series of exchanges that had started on a flirtatious note but had become more heated as she scrolled up to the top.

"What are you doing?"

Nesta looked up to see Catrin's horrified face. The feeling of betrayal was clear.

"I'm not surprised you didn't tell me," said Nesta.

Catrin snatched the phone away. "I don't know what you're talking about."

"How long had it been going on for? This affair... weeks? Months? Fifteen years?" Her last estimate caused the other woman to nearly drop her phone. "Was Dafydd still in school when it started? He would have been in sixth form back then."

The shock had quickly turned to anger. "You have no idea what you're talking about. It wasn't like that."

"No?" Nesta sat back in her chair. "You know, I asked Dafydd's father — our old headteacher — about the time you reported his son's behaviour. When you saw that he was bullying Arwel Maddocks. Dyfrig had no memory of it, and that man has a memory like an elephant." She gave the younger woman a harsh stare. "You didn't report it, did you? What a strange thing to lie about. And it got me thinking. This affair had been going on longer than I could have imagined."

"Like I said — you don't know what you're talking about."

"How about you help me understand?" Nesta asked. "Why didn't you go to Dyfrig all those years ago?"

"I decided to take matters into my own hands," Catrin snapped. "I couldn't just go to the young man's father. So, I asked Dafydd to stay behind after school one day." She sat herself down. "I really gave him a piece of my mind that day. It was like confronting my own bully. And he just stared at me the whole time, like he was enjoying it. By the time I had finished, this strange feeling came over me — like I'd enjoyed it myself. As the weeks went on, his behaviour in my classes got worse. It was as if he was *trying* to stay back after class. He was different from all of the other pupils. He seemed to have this maturity beyond his years." Catrin shook her head in shame. "I was practically a teenager myself back then. There was barely an age gap."

Nesta gave her a judgmental glare. "But he *was* a pupil, and you were a teacher."

"Don't you think I know that?!" Catrin tried to remain calm. "There was this strange chemistry between us. He could sense it, too. The lad was in sixth form by then — he'd turned eighteen for crying out loud! He was basically an adult."

The older woman sighed. "How long did it go on for?"

"It stopped as soon as he graduated and left for university," said Catrin. "That was how brief it was. We never kept in touch or anything like that. It was never spoken of again."

"But then he came back," said Nesta.

Catrin clutched her mouth to hold in a sob. "I was a different person by the time he joined as a teacher. I'd even tried to block the whole thing out of my mind like it had never happened. I wasn't a young teacher anymore — I was a deputy head — a married woman."

"Dafydd's situation had changed a lot by then, too. It must have been quite awkward on his first day."

"I was petrified," said Catrin. "I never wanted him to get the job in the first place. But Johnny was adamant. Him and Dafydd went *way* back. There was no convincing him. But, then, the strangest thing happened." The deputy head became distant for a moment, as she re-lived the moment Dafydd came back into her life. "We bumped into each other on his first day, and he acted like nothing had ever happened. I was initially relieved, obviously, but, as the days went by, I became disappointed. Those feelings had clearly never gone away."

"*Feelings*?" Nesta asked. She didn't hide her cynicism. "Are you sure you weren't mixing up feelings with lust? Don't go telling me you were actually in *love* with this man?"

Catrin shook her head. "I can't say what it was. Either way, my career and marriage was far more important by this point. But, then, one day, he cornered me in the geography classroom. I'd taught a class that day and nobody was around. He closed the door and began pouring his heart out to me. He said he hadn't stopped thinking about me since the day he left Bala." She felt an onset of tears and tried to stop them. "He said that I was the reason he'd come back — he wanted to finish what we started all those years ago."

"And what did you say?"

"Very little at first. I was shocked. Eventually, he pinned me against the wall and started kissing me, but I pushed him away. He was shocked too, but then I started shouting at him, threatening him. The more I yelled, the more he seemed to enjoy it. He was like a pupil all over again."

"You weren't tempted by him?"

"No!" Catrin cried. "Well, I was still attracted to him, obviously, but I'm not stupid. I ended up slapping him and telling him to never approach me like that again. And he didn't. Shortly afterwards, he began a brief affair with the drama teacher. He wasn't subtle about it. The whole thing was his way of trying to make me jealous."

Nesta nodded. "Did it work?"

"Of course not! I'm a grown woman!"

"Those early messages on your phone would imply otherwise." Nesta pointed towards her mobile.

Catrin sighed. "When he realised his attempts to make me jealous weren't working, he got hold of my number. I ignored his messages at first, but, one night, I'd drunk too much wine and started responding. It was stupid, but we had a whole back and forth the entire night."

A disgusted Nesta listened with no great surprise. She had read those early messages, and they had been steamier than any of the spicy romance novels she had read so far.

"I woke up the next day and regretted it," Catrin continued. "The messages were still there and made me feel terrible. I never responded after that. It must have driven him nuts." She walked over to the large window overlooking her back garden. The conservatory was still under construction and building materials were scattered everywhere. "Weeks went by, and the next minute, he was at my front door. We argued and then… one thing led to another."

"You slept with each other?" Nesta asked.

"It all happened so quickly. I don't know what came over me!" Catrin turned around and gasped. "Hywel…"

Standing in the doorway was her husband. The man in stained work clothes glared at his wife in disbelief. "You're unbelievable," he hissed.

"It was a mistake," Catrin pleaded, rushing over to him. She tried to grab his hands, but he pulled them away.

"Get away from me!" Hywel roared. He moved to the opposite side of the kitchen and tried to process what he had just overheard. "You said he'd been harassing you. You said he'd come here to try and —" The man couldn't bring himself to finish his sentence and let out a sob. After clearing his throat, the despair had turned to anger. "What have you done?!"

"He tried to threaten me!"

Catrin's cry echoed around the kitchen, but there didn't seem to be much sympathy from her listeners.

"How did it happen?" Nesta asked.

Hywel saw the look on the older woman's face. He knew exactly what she was asking. "Are you going to tell her?" the man asked his wife. "Tell her what you *did*?"

"I don't know what you're talking about," Catrin snapped.

"She knows!" Hywel cried. "And I'm sick of lying for you!" He rubbed his sore eyes. "All this time... you played me for a fool. You deserve to be locked up!"

"Hywel, stop!"

Nesta ignored Catrin's cries of protest. "You know," she said. "I realised recently that I've never seen your car, Catrin. Like me, you probably hardly need to use it. Everything in town is within walking distance. That garage door of yours is always closed. But something tells me that you drive a blue *Renault Clio*. The same one spotted down by the lake that night along with Dafydd's car."

Catrin was horrified.

"You see!" Hywel cried. "I told you — she knows! You were never going to get away with it, Catrin. And I won't let you drag me down with you..."

His wife wanted to drop to her knees. She turned back around to face the window. "It all happened so quickly." Catrin stared at the small building site outside and pictured Dafydd standing there, amongst the tools and rubble, as he had been the day he died. "He came around again, thinking we would have the same experience as last time. But he was wrong. I told him to leave, and when he started kissing me, I slapped him. Once he realised that I was serious, his mood changed. He seemed genuinely cross and frustrated — almost heartbroken. I said, if he ever came around again, I'd call the police on him. I even threatened to get him sacked so I'd never have to see him at school. That's when it really sunk in for him." She continued to stare at her back garden. "We were outside when it happened. Dafydd started reminding me of the fact that he was a school pupil when all of this first started. He said, if anyone from the school found out about what we did back then, my career would be over. And he was right. I'd never be able to work again. Then there was my marriage..." Her husband's reflection was now visible in the glass, and she saw his distraught face. "He threatened to tell Hywel and sacrifice his own relationship just to hurt me. I could tell he meant it, too. For whatever reason, he'd become obsessed. I knew it would never be over whilst he was still around." Catrin could see the paving stones that Dafydd had been standing on. "He had his back turned, and I panicked. He said it was a shame that my conservatory would never be finished unless I admitted my true feelings for him. He was literally blackmailing me into some twisted relationship. So, I picked up the hammer from Hywel's toolbox, and, before he turned around, I smashed the back of his head with every ounce of strength I had left."

Nesta closed her eyes and grimaced. No matter how vile or detestable a person had been, she could never imagine taking someone's life. She'd even had some pupils in her time that she would have quite happily choked on occasion, but Nesta had spent her career seeing the potential in *everyone*. As naive as that may have been, and as much as her own husband had ridiculed her for it, she needed that sense of hope in her life. The thought of Dafydd Thomas, that former student who sat at the back of her class, being struck down in such a brutal fashion chilled her to the very core.

Catrin was still deep in her recollection, and tears began streaming down her face. "I never imagined killing anyone," she said. "But, at that moment, I felt like I had no choice."

"Everyone has a choice," said Nesta.

"I didn't know what else to do!" The younger woman turned around and looked over at her husband. "That's when Hywel walked in."

Hywel's breathing had become very heavy. His entire body was now trembling. "She told me that she'd killed him in self-defence," he said. "I was so shocked, I believed her. She begged me to help her get rid of him. We knew that both of her lives would be changed forever if we called the police. So I suggested that we take his car and park it somewhere remote. He stank of alcohol. People would think he had just drunk too much and hit his head."

"After being hit by a *hammer*?" Nesta asked. She was beginning to suspect that her former protégé had not been as smart as she had initially given her credit for. Either that, or she had been very desperate for a solution.

Catrin shrugged. "Even if they suspected anything," she said. "There was no way for them to connect it back to me."

"I beg to differ," Nesta muttered.

"We drove down there in separate cars," said Hywel. "That probably wasn't the cleverest move, but it's easy to judge in hindsight, especially when you're not going through it. We weren't thinking straight. I was still fuming about what Dafydd had tried to do to my wife." He looked over at Catrin and his lip began to tremble. "I never imagined that he was actually her *lover*."

"He was *not* my lover!" Catrin screamed.

"Call it what you want," said her husband. "After dumping

the car and the body, I disposed of the hammer and did a clean-up of the back garden. We were ready to carry on with the rest of our lives."

Nesta looked out at the early foundations of a conservatory. Personally, she would have found it very difficult to enjoy her back garden knowing that a brutal murder had taken place, but she supposed that everyone was different.

"You won't tell anyone will you, Nesta?"

Catrin's pleading eyes made the older woman want to be sick. She was loyal to all of her friends and could keep a secret like the best of them. But this secret was an entirely different kettle of fish.

"She won't have to," said Hywel. The two women both turned to look at him. "I'll tell the police myself."

His wife burst into tears, and Nesta decided that she had more than outstayed her welcome. In the course of a single day, she had found answers to the questions that had been plaguing her for weeks but had also lost a close friend in the process. Just like everything else in her life, people came and went.

Nesta left the house on Trem Y Ffridd road with only a slight feeling of closure. Unlike her private library of murder mystery books, perhaps that *this* mystery was better left unsolved. Fiction, it seemed, was a lot less close to home.

CHAPTER 26

The surface of Llyn Tegid was pink from the falling sun. The light was fading fast, but there was just enough time for one last walk before the day was out.

Nesta Griffiths followed her Jack Russell along the water's edge, as she had done for many years. The only difference this time was that she was joined by another companion. Unlike Hari, this person did not not bear a shaggy coat or move around on four legs. Instead, he was covered up by a black *Iron Maiden* hoodie and possessed footwear that was far from suitable for a walk beside the lake.

"I *did* offer my spare pair of wellies," said Nesta, watching the teenager scrubbing his *Converse* trainers against a patch of grass.

Darren Price ignored the comment and wiped off a piece of dog muck. "I bet you that was him," he said, pointing to the Jack Russell jumping around in the water.

Nesta was rather insulted. "I'll have you know that I bag and bin *all* of my waste, thank you very much."

The disgusted young man shuddered and decided that such an activity was even worse. "You *really* do this everyday?" he asked, shivering.

"Of course," said Nesta.

"Why?" Darren asked.

The retired teacher stared out at the view and took in a deep breath of fresh air. "Well, first of all, Hari needs his exercise. Second of all, I need mine. And thirdly… there's something about a good walk that clears my head."

The teenager shook his own head in disapproval. "You should buy a treadmill." He looked over towards the area where Dafydd Thomas had been found not that long ago. "Guess it's unlikely you'll find another body now. Can't believe it was a teacher." Darren gave it some more thought. "Actually, I *can* believe it. But not *that* teacher. Maybe like a maths teacher or something."

"Nobody was more surprised than me," said Nesta, gazing at a gaggle of wild geese up in the distance.

"At least we got to find out," said Darren. "It was killing me. I was sure it was the fiancée." He turned to her with a smile. "Guess you must be the Welsh version of that Belgium detective."

Nesta chuckled. "A Welsh-Belgian detective? Now *that* would be a strange thing. I'd say Miss Marple is a better comparison at my age."

"Who?"

"Never mind."

Darren picked up a stone and threw it as far as he could into the water. He watched it land with a slight element of pride.

"I bet you can't do *that* on your *Play-Box*," said Nesta.

"*Play-Box*?" The amused teenager rolled his eyes. "Oh, sure. This is way more fun than video games." Nesta picked up her own stone and managed to skim it across the water multiple times. Darren was very impressed but tried not to show it.

"So," he said. "Do you think you'll carry on teaching now?"

The woman beside him gave his question some serious

thought. She had been considering her future for a few days now. With Catrin gone and her old colleagues dropping like flies to the allure of retirement, she was beginning to deliberate hanging up her chalk and ruler for good. "Who knows. Maybe, I'll just take up painting, instead."

"*Painting*?!"

Nesta shrugged. "People seem to find it relaxing." She thought about art teacher Martin Edwards and his fiery temper. "Not *everyone*, mind, but some. Or I might even take up the piano again. Get some proper lessons."

Darren groaned. "Wow. I guess retirement's as boring as it looks."

"Yes," said Nesta. "I suppose it is when you haven't got a murder investigation on the go."

They both smiled at each other.

"I'm sure you won't have to wait long," said Darren. "You know what people around here are like."

All of a sudden, the teenager noticed a shift in the retired teacher's demeanour. Something up in the distance had caught her attention, and she seemed a little frazzled.

"Does my hair look alright?" she asked, patting down her scalp. "The wind's a bit stronger this evening."

Darren looked over his shoulder to see an older man walking his Newfoundland up in the distance. He saw his friend's nervous glances and a large grin crept across his face. "Oh, yeah? The *wind* is bothering you, is it? Sure it's not something else?" The young man pointed towards Dai Green and winked at her.

"Don't be so silly," she snapped.

"So, *this* is why you come down here every day!" Darren began puckering his lips and blowing wolf whistles.

Nesta *hushed* him. "Will you be quiet! You're embarrassing me now. What you're suggesting is absolutely outrageous!" She was just about to poke him with her umbrella, when Dai called out her name. "Oh, hello, Dai!" she called back and lifted up her hand for an awkward wave.

"Well," said Darren. "What are you waiting for?" She looked at him, dumbfounded by his question. "Aren't you going to ask the guy out for a drink or something?"

The retired woman scoffed and shook her head. "You young people have no idea."

Darren frowned. "What was it you told me? Not to miss an opportunity when it's staring you in the face? Before it's too late?"

"Did I really say that?" asked Nesta.

The young man shrugged. "I don't know. Something like that. I wasn't really listening."

Nesta tutted him and walked away. She made the long journey over to where Dai Green was busy throwing his dog a stick.

"Dai," she said. "Good to see you again."

"Likewise," said Dai. "We really have to stop meeting like this!" He let out a chuckle.

The woman in front of him was preparing herself for the big question. "Actually," she said. "There was something I forgot to ask you last time."

"Really?" Dai chucked another stick away and turned to her. "Well, a lot has happened since we last met. I take it you heard about Dafydd Thomas' killer?"

Nesta nodded. "Oh, yes. Shocking, wasn't it? Never saw *that* one coming."

"I had an inkling it was one of the teachers," said Dai. "Mine were nasty pieces of work when I was in school. Especially that headmaster."

"Is that right," said Nesta. "So, you fancy yourself a private detective, Dai? Like in those murder mystery books?"

The man's face soured. "Murder mysteries?" He snorted. "Heavens, no. I can't stand murder mystery books. They're too predictable and far-fetched. Give me a non-fiction book anyday. Fiction is a complete waste of time in my opinion."

"You really think so?"

"Well, it's all just made up, isn't it? Where's the fun in that?"

Nesta watched him laugh and felt her heart begin to break. Her face was horrified, as she endured a rare moment of speechlessness.

Over in the distance, Darren was watching the entire exchange whilst playing with Hari. He waited, patiently, until Nesta returned with a weary expression.

"Well?" he asked. "How did it go?"

The woman shook her head. "Change of plan. I think I'll have to give this one a miss."

"Fair enough," said Darren. "Plenty more fish in the sea. Talking of which — fancy grabbing some fish and chips from *Badell*?"

Nesta smiled. "I think that's a marvellous idea."

Hari the Jack Russell chased after them, as they both made their way back across the wet ground.

"Hey," said Darren, as they approached the main road heading back into town. "Did you hear about that body they found in Corwen?"

Nesta had not heard about this latest incident and listened with great interest. The town of Corwen was less than fifteen miles away, and she had a strange feeling that the next phase of her retirement was going to be anything but "boring". She looked up to see the streetlights of Bala High Street flicker into life, and Nesta smiled, as darkness began to descend on her beloved hometown.

ABOUT THE AUTHOR

We hope you enjoyed this book. Reviews are extremely important for new authors, so please do feel free to write a short review on the book's Amazon page.

Whilst you're waiting for Book 2 in this new series, why not try the first book in another P. L Handley murder mystery series:

The Murder Ledger
By P. L. Handley
Available on Amazon

If you'd like to read more books in this new series, you can join the P. L. Handley e-mail newsletter and receive all the latest news on future releases.

Subscribe to the e-mailing list by visiting the official P. L. Handley website at: www.plhandley.com

Printed in Great Britain
by Amazon